SCUM OF THE EARTH

The business district below Columbus Circle at night is a place for prowlers, rapists, muggers, a place where cops in patrol cars go by fast so they don't see trouble, and if they do, sometimes, eyes are closed, heads look the other way and cars travel faster.

Our free catalogue is available upon request. Any Leisure Books title not in your local bookstore can be purchased through the mail. Simply send 25¢ plus the retail price of the books to Nordon Publications, Inc., 185 Madison Avenue, New York, N.Y. 10016.

Any titles currently in print are available in quantity for industry and sales promotion use at reduced rate. Address inquiries to our Promotion Department.

Ryker

THE SADIST

Edson T. Hamill

LEISURE BOOKS • NEW YORK CITY

A LEISURE BOOK

Published by

Nordon Publications, Inc.
185 Madison Avenue
New York, New York 10016

Copyright ᶜ 1975 by Nordon Publications, Inc.

All rights reserved.
Printed in the United States of America.

Chapter One

The business district below Columbus Circle at night is a place for prowlers, rapists, muggers, a place where cops in patrol cars go by fast so they don't see trouble and if they do, sometimes eyes are closed, heads look the other way and cars travel faster.

The Anslow Building had been put up in the twenties. The once elegant red sandstone gargoyles, seraphs and angels now looked gauche. The light red had turned to dark brown. Gray and black stuck to the corners and edges.

Some of the offices still showed yellow light. In some

peals of laughter drifted out into the cold winter night. The sun was setting and darkness crept in from the Hudson.

Betty Marcel looked at her face in the compact mirror. Not bad, she thought—few lines, some crows' feet around the eyes. She was no longer young, but over the years she had taken care of herself.

A woman who didn't watch herself could lose her husband. When she thought about this, tears appeared at the corners of her eyes. For the last six months her husband Edward had been staying late at the office, sometimes not coming home till four or five in the morning. He never offered any excuse. If she asked, he mentioned that he had work to do. She could see through this and he knew it, and he didn't care that she knew. That hurt worst of all.

Putting the compact back in her bag, she rose and got her coat from the wooden hanger tree in the corner of the cavernous office. All the others had gone home. The covers were on the typewriters and the place looked desolate.

Her boss had asked Betty to stay and do some extra correspondence. She had agreed, not so much because she felt like working, but because it would mean she would get home later. The less she saw of her house, empty, silent rooms, the better.

She put on her coat and tied a gay yellow scarf around her dark red hair, lightly streaked with gray. It wasn't the kind of scarf one wore with a drab brown coat, but she felt like having something bright, something that said "Look, I'm alive."

She looked around to make sure she had left nothing behind and locked up the office. She walked quickly down the deserted hall past the dark pebbled glass doorways on either side.

She rang for the elevator and waited, listening to the wheeze of overworked motors, then the door rattled open and she stepped inside. A faint musty smell rose from the shaft below as the car descended.

The lobby was deserted except for a tall man in a dark gray coat. He held an attache case and seemed to be waiting for someone. She paid him scant attention as she pushed open the outside door, but in the brief instant she had looked at him, his odd, almost animal-like eyes registered on her brain. Then she was moving along the sidewalk toward the end of the block, heading north to Columbus Circle and the subway.

The man waited only till she had passed outside, then followed. This was his woman, his hit. In the attache case was a forty-five automatic. The bullets in the chamber and the clip were snub-nosed, soft lead. The heads had been crossed with a sharp knife. He had done the job himself the night before. She would get three—one in the head, one in the chest, one in the back. She might be alive when she hit the sidewalk, but she would not make it to a hospital alive—and that was important.

Betty Marcel looked back and saw him coming. He was looking at her, and she thought again of his eyes. These were not the eyes of a living man, but of someone dead inside. He was coming faster now, only fifteen feet behind.

She began to walk more quickly, but he did not speed up. She was safe. She was in the open where people could see. He would not dare to rape her. But if he tried, would anyone stop him? This was New York, the big, heartless city.

She had tried to keep panic from rising by the idea that people were around, but when she looked they were the only two on the street. She walked faster, her heart racing, her mind frantic.

She looked back. He was forty feet behind. The end of the block was a hundred feet ahead. Then the streetlights came on all at once. It was like being under a searchlight. Now the street on both sides was bathed in light. The lights burned pink and gave the dark streets a strange glow. His face, when she turned to look, had taken on a demon aspect.

He was smiling now. She could not go on, there was no place to run. Her mind was half mad with fear. This man was not a rapist. This was not the face of lust, but the face of death. She did not know how, but she was certain of this.

Then she saw an open door that led into another office building. Here surely was someone who could give her refuge. She opened the door and ran inside. She was gasping, her eyes a wild blur in her white face.

She ran down the marble lobby to the elevator, her footsteps echoing. The door was opening. She pressed the elevator button and looked up at the metal arrow that went around a semi-circle with numbers set in it. The elevator, like the one in her building, wheezed slowly down from the ninth floor.

She looked back. He was near the door, standing there staring at her, the attache case in his hand, his face a caricature of death.

It seemed like a bad dream, but it was as real as the marble floor under her feet. The elevator was on the fifth floor now. He began to walk towards her.

Fearfully she ran toward the fire stairs and pulled at the heavy door. It resisted, but two good jerks got it open. She ran into the stairwell and started up the concrete stairs, using the dusty iron handrail to pull herself up.

She went up the grimy, foul-smelling stairs that had not been cleaned in a long time. She ran on, her breath was coming in jerking gasps.

In the lobby, the man waited for the elevator, and when

he stepped inside pushed the button for the sixth floor. No use running and tiring himself out. A true professional, he was logical, calm, and collected. When the elevator stopped and the door opened, he stepped out into the hall and headed for the fire stairs.

Unless she was an extremely calm and confident woman, she would keep running up in the mistaken belief he was hot on her trail.

When he opened the door she was coming up the steps. Her mouth fell open and she froze in her place. When he began coming down toward her, she turned to run down.

Confused, sweating, exhausted, out of breath, she stumbled and fell down six steps, striking her teeth and head. Bloody and dazed, she came to a stop.

When she was able to struggle into a sitting position, she looked up and saw him standing over her, the suitcase in his hand.

"Who are you? What do you want?" She found her voice.

He pointed to himself and answered with a faint smile. "I am death. You are my victim."

"Why?"

"For money, dear lady. For twenty thousand dollars."

"But—who?" She looked at him bewildered, unable to comprehend the full horror.

"Can't you guess? Your beloved husband. The one who promised to love, honor and cherish. He wishes to be rid of you, not to have to pay alimony. He wishes to be free. There is another woman."

"Let me go, I won't ask for alimony."

"So you say. But you have seen me. I'm sorry, I never go back on a hit. Get up."

Numbly she rose, dusting off her hands. It seemed ludicrous even to her, but in the arms of death people do strange things.

He stepped aside. "Up the stairs. Walk fast. I'll tell you when to stop." She began, and he followed close behind. She hoped against hope, but she knew no savior would open a fire door and step out on the stairs. Such dramatic rescues were found only in the movies.

She didn't feel tired or even scared after the first few flights, just numb. Little details like cobwebs in dark corners registered in her mind. His shoes creaked on the concrete steps.

On the tenth floor he told her to stop. "I'm tired," he explained as he took off his hat and wiped sweat from his forehead. His black hair was tousled. He seemed strangely human at that moment, not at all like a killer. Then he put his hat on again and his face took on an impassive set.

"Okay, walk." She began to climb again. It was hard, but she dared not stop. On the thirteenth floor, an unlucky number, she stopped and said, "I'll give you anything—money, sex—please don't kill me."

He smiled pleasantly, amused by her pathetic offer. He shook his head and said, "Money I'll get from your husband. Can you offer me twenty thousand?" She shook her head. "Besides, if I did take it, my rep would go. No rep, no jobs. Sorry. As for sex, I don't think you're quite my type."

Spurred on by fear she climbed to the top floor without any strain. A diamond chain link door stood between them and the roof stairs. A padlock was on the door and it held a length of chain, locked tight.

He opened the attache case, took out a lock cutter and put it around the steel bar holding the lock shut. He pressed down and there was a metallic snap. The padlock and chain were easily removed.

She noticed he wore light, transparent plastic gloves on

his hands. He turned to her. "A lot of times we have to go up on the roof. A lock cutter comes in handy."

He opened the door and waved at the stairs. "You first." She smelled his pine scented cologne. It smelled good, she thought as she went past him up the steps. Was he going to kill her here?

When they reached the roof he pushed open the door and motioned her out. The roof was tar covered, with ventilation ducts and pipes and a central structure that ended in a large smokestack.

The roof was deserted. He made her walk along the edge with him. As she stared out over the great mass of buildings her heart trembled in fear that he would toss her over.

She would plunge to her death, and she wasn't strong enough to fight him. Fear had made her numb, sapping all her energy.

Many of the nearby buildings were higher than this one, and she could see faces in windows across the way, some looking at them on the roof. She wanted to shout at them, call for help, but knew that too was futile. He would have her over the edge in a second and be gone. No one could stop him or get help to her in time, even if they heard. This was one heartless town, Edward always said. She thought of what this man had said about Edward. She thought of telling her husband she would never speak to him again. How foolish after what he was having done to her. How stupid, she chided herself. She wasn't going to be talking to anyone. That's what this man was hired for—a professional murderer. Her life was about to be snuffed out, and all she could think about were petty subjects.

She tried to reason with the killer once again, even though she knew it was futile. "Please don't kill me. Have a heart."

"Don't beg, my dear. I hate it when they beg. They die

even more horrible deaths if they do that. Over the years I've learned to hate that more than anything. You're dead and that's it. You aren't going anyplace. Just don't make trouble. I'll make it quick and you won't suffer."

He looked up at the chimney and pulled her away from the edge. For a moment her heart gave a little leap of joy. He wasn't going to kill her. Then she realized he had seen a better way than tossing her down to the street below.

He had seen a way that would be quick and quiet. There was sweat on the sides of his face and he opened his mouth to take in air. She still did not realize why she was noticing such things now. He had two dull gold teeth on the left side of his mouth.

He was taking her to a series of platforms in the middle section of the roof. So far he had not taken out a gun. He didn't need one. His manner was enough of a threat. He did not need to show her any kind of weapon, but there was one handy if he needed it.

He put down his attache case. "See those iron rungs in the brick wall, going up to the first level? I want you to climb them. I'll be right behind."

"Why?"

"Don't be foolish, woman. You know not to ask me questions. I don't answer, I just give orders and you follow them. Be a good girl. Go up those steps before I get mad."

She trembled, then turned away from him and began to climb, finding it difficult in platform shoes. At last she made it to the next level, clambered up on hands and knees and struggled to stand. She looked back and saw him coming up, leaning his attache case on the roof.

She looked over his head at the city laid out before her eyes. It was almost as beautiful as on the post cards they sold in Rockefeller Center. When she had first come to the city from Scranton, she had been fascinated by the size of

New York and had always written home to her parents and sisters on post cards she bought at Rockefeller Center. Many times they were skyline photos, and now the skyline was like something in another world.

He got up onto the platform, dusted off his pants and said, "The next rung ladder—take it. We're going higher." She wanted to refuse but could not.

"Move a little faster, my dear." He was smiling, his gold teeth showing. She climbed up onto the next level. The height was making her dizzy. Betty had always been afraid of heights, but it hadn't bothered her until this moment. Her fear had kept that phobia from taking control.

Now she was no longer afraid of death. She was numb—it was a calming numbness.

He climbed up behind her. She thought of running to the edge and kicking him in the face so he would fall down, but how far could he fall? Five or six feet—not enough to hurt him. He would just get angry, come back up and throw her off. Wasn't that what he was going to do anyway? She wasn't sure. There was still the hope that perhaps he would not kill her. Perhaps he was attracted to her and had taken her up here where he could rape her and run away.

When he had climbed up and dusted himself off again he stepped up to her and said, "There's only one more set of rungs. Start climbing. Time's a wastin'." She wanted to hesitate, but again she nodded and began to climb. She had lost all will to fight.

To the hit man this was no surprise. He had witnessed this reaction before. How long it took to set in depended on the woman, but they all caved in before the end.

She climbed the last rung, almost slipping once and again he came up after her. There was a platform in the center and coming up out of it were twin smokestacks.

He chose the one nearest to them. It was about three

feet high, just above her waist. Taking her by the upper arm, he guided her towards it.

"Look down in the smokestack." She hesitated, looked at him with tear-filled eyes, now that she knew what he was planning. She shook her head.

"Come on," he said, tugging her and putting some meanness into his voice. That always made them move. She moved till the edge of the chimney was digging into her belly.

"Look down. Tell me what you see." She looked and gasped. It was a narrow, unending shaft, its walls edged with grime.

"It's like a well, isn't it? Never ending." A shiver started in her face, traveled down her neck and along her body to the ankles and back up.

"This is where you will die." He smiled and his two gold teeth gleamed. His face seemed to take on a life it had not had before, as if he were absorbing her life before it was taken from her body.

He held her by both wrists and pulled her forward. He walked around the chimney so he stood across from her on the other side, holding onto her wrists all the while.

Between them the open chimney mouth waited. A thin column of smoke rose from deep inside. The boilers were starting up. The hot gray smoke made the air between them shimmer.

He pulled her forward and moved back from the chimney. He left her no opening. She wanted to flee now, but fear was taking all resistance out of her.

She could not run, could not move away. All at once he let go of her wrists and clamped down on her elbows, holding them in an iron grip. Her strength was ebbing as much from fear as from strain.

Again, he let go of her and grabbed her by the shoulders.

He pressed so hard with his fingers she thought they would go through her flesh.

Now that he had a good grip on her he pulled forward. His face was red with the effort, sweat running down it in glistening trails. He now had her bent almost double over the chimney. Her face was in the thickening stream and she was inhaling too much smoke. She coughed and choked and her body wracked with spasms.

Pressing down harder, he held and forced her forward another few inches. The smoke was also running into his face and making him cough. He shook his head and continued to pull.

Holding onto one of her shoulders, he put his other hand atop her head and pressed down hard. She resisted, but by then the fear, the draining of her reserves, the smoke in her lungs, had all taken their toll. Her head sunk lower and lower and soon was below the inner edge of the chimney.

He let go of her shoulder, grabbed her upper back with both hands and pulled down and forward. She was dizzy with the smoke. It was coming out past the stricture of her body and across her face in thick clouds. He coughed and turned his head to the side.

He tilted her in and felt her legs come up off the platform into the air. As she tipped over into the chimney well, he was able to slide her over the edge. He looked directly at her, held her for a second and let go.

A soul rending wail escaped her throat and followed her down the shaft.

He looked down and watched her fall as she grew smaller and smaller. The fall wasn't clean—she bumped against the walls, slid for dozen feet, fell free, then slid again, became wedged for a second, slid and fell. Her screams came up at him like echoes. He smiled as the smoke swallowed her up. It was over and done with. It had been a good job. Not one of his cleaner ones, but a good job. Michael Marlin had just earned twenty thousand dollars.

He leaned back against the chimney and watched the smoke float off into the night sky. Then he stuck a cigarette in his mouth and lit it.

Chapter Two

The phone rang like an insistent gong in the silence of the den. Its sound traveled from one end of the book-lined room to the other. The man at the far end rose from his comfortable chair and took his pipe from his mouth. A glass of sherry was in one hand a new book in the other.

The phone rang again. He put down the book, placed the glass on an oak table and strode over to the telephone table. "Hello, who is this?"

"A friend." The voice stroked his ear like silk.

"This you, Marlin?" he asked in a suddenly edgy voice.

"The one and only. This is the call you've been waiting for. Relax. The mission is accomplished. You're free. Now you mourn a little, shed some crocodile tears for your wife and then marry this new bimbo."

Marcel's temper rose. "Don't call her that." Then he stopped. Why argue with a gunman, a common hired killer?

Before he could say any more, Marlin answered, "Sorry. I forgot myself. I didn't call about that. I called about the money. You have it?"

"Sure I do. You didn't think I'd make a deal and not keep it?"

"In my line, Marcel, you think of everything. People try all sorts of tricks. I had one who thought he'd be smarter than me. He threatened me. Imagine that. A guy has to be pretty stupid to threaten a hired gun, but he did. You know what he told me?"

"No, what?" Marcel asked, fascinated.

"He says, I'm not going to give you twenty thousand. I don't have it. I lied. You are a killer. I'll tell the police. They'll arrest you. So you'd better be far away by morning. I was, but only after I shot him dead on the sidewalk in front of his house. It only happened once. I make sure to tell all my clients about that one time. They make sure they don't wind up like he did."

"Wait a second, Marlin. I wasn't thinking that way. You don't have to threaten me. I'll come through. I always do. I promised and I'll pay. When do you want it?" He could almost see Marlin smile at the other end.

"Tomorrow. Remember how I want it?"

"Sure, I remember. Fifties. Four hundred of them, in five-thousand-dollar packets. New and crisp."

"Right. A pound of new money. There are twenty-six bills to an ounce. Did you know that? Four hundred bills is almost a pound. I'll be waiting eagerly for it. This hit was no breeze."

"She is dead?" Marcel asked, tension in his voice.

"Where I put her, she won't come back."

"How are you sure?"

"I'm sure. It's one of those habits you develop in this line. I'm very sure."

"How did she go, a bullet, two bullets?"

"Mr. Marcel," he said, suddenly formal, "don't ask. Sometimes a man hires me to kill his wife and then gets to feeling sorry. Only, there's nothing he can do. You can't bring back the dead. You tell a man how she went, it sometimes affects his head. So don't ask. It's better for you and me. Good day, Mr. Marcel. I'll call tomorrow. You'll be home the usual time?"

"Yes. The usual time."

"Goodbye then, Mr. Marcel."

"Goodbye, Marlin." The phone went dead before Marcel could say more. He dropped it back in the cradle like something hot and rancid. Then he looked around the dimly lit room with the books and the rich Persian carpet on the floor and wished he had never met Michael Marlin.

Detective Sergeant Joe Ryker cursed when the phone rang in his Manhattan apartment and disturbed his late supper. He put down his sandwich and went to answer it.

There was a new homicide. A woman had been pushed through the roof smokestack of the Arnborn Building near Columbus Circle. She had fallen into the boiler and had begun burning. The night attendant noticed a smell of scorched flesh, shut the boiler and opened it up. He saw the partially destroyed body and called the police.

"I'll be down," was all he said before he hung up. He got his green trench coat, locked up and went to get his car. He headed for the 21st Precinct House on West 68th Street and mounted the dilapidated gray stone steps. He nodded at the desk sergeant as he walked by to the stairs.

The Detective Division Homicide Squad room looked seedy as usual. He sometimes expected it to change in the few hours he was away, but no such luck. Ryker waved at a few of the others and stepped up to the cubicle that belonged to Lieutenant Sal Fischetti and knocked.

"Come in," a voice shouted. Fischetti gave him a sour look and pointed to the hard wood chair in front of his cluttered gray steel desk. "Sit your skinny ass down, Joe. A new murder."

"So I heard, Sal. When do we see the body?"

"You sound gleeful."

"I'm never gleeful, Sal. I just like to see the body. Sometimes the way the job is done gives you an insight into the mind of the murderer. You know how it is."

"Yes, I know." Fischetti stared at him, still unable to understand this hard, sometimes cold man. He was not like the others in many ways. Fischetti both hated and liked him, yet treated Ryker with a special respect. Ryker wasn't one to kowtow or kiss ass.

"The body is over at the Bellevue morgue. We can go there if you want."

"Any idea who the broad is?"

"Identification was destroyed in the furnace. We're having her teeth X-rays checked, and two fingers were burned only lightly. Prints have been taken. We sent them off to our central file and to Washington. We ought to know by two a.m."

"Good, I'll be glad for anything we can get. How's Connolly? He know about this yet?"

Fischetti shook his head. Connolly was the Deputy Inspector, his boss and Ryker's. He was the man who gave orders when you got down to details.

"I'd like to go up on the roof of this building where she was pushed."

"We'll go there after we hit Bellevue," Fischetti answered. He got up from his desk and reached to the clothes tree behind him to get his jacket. When he put this on over his shirt, he hid his gun and shoulder holster.

As they went downstairs and out, Ryker wondered if this was some new maniac, one of the breed that periodically infested the city, or a mob hit man, as usually turned out to be the case. In those instances the cops prayed the violence would end and merely catalogued the murders as they came along. Asked about it, they would say they were investigating new leads and hoped for a solution soon.

Fischetti went to the Chrysler parked around the corner and got in. He unlocked the opposite door and Ryker slid in. They pulled out and drove south on Broadway. Hookers lined the bright spots and the shadows, depending on their eagerness for clients. Pimps rode by in flashy cars. Lincoln Tower and the lower class Amsterdam Houses were almost side by side. Lincoln Center was just blocks from sleazy sex shows. The rich and the poor rubbed shoulders on the wide sidewalks by day and night, with the poor practicing their own version of redistribution of wealth by mugging those foolish enough to walk the streets after dark.

Ryker hated the high class fools and the turgid of the poor. He hated the hard core porno, with gaudy displays of perverted sex.

He closed his eyes and thought about his dinner that night and the emptiness of his apartment. There was just the job and the money. It was the only living Ryker knew or cared about. Murder was his main interest in life and getting petty punks behind bars his only mission.

There were people who liked the safety and security of a nine to five job. His security was seeing the streets of

Manhattan wiped clean of the scum who molested citizens and visitors.

He opened his eyes and looked at the streets flying by. Fischetti was driving crosstown now. "How's the wife?" Ryker asked out of nowhere, just to make conversation.

"Viola's all right. Why do you ask?"

"You told me you'd been worried about her flu."

Fischetti cast a withering glance at Ryker. "That was three months back. Nice time for you to remember."

Ryker cursed himself inwardly. Instead of getting close to Fischetti he had made himself look like a fool. He didn't say any more till they hit Bellevue on the Lower East Side.

They flashed their buzzers and the gate man let them in. They parked and entered the main building, headed for the emergency room and showed their cards and badges. A young intern appeared and told them to follow him.

People sat here in various stages of dress. Some were on stretchers, others moaned in pain, some were getting intravenous solutions, blood or medication. A few had bandages. Nurses rushed about with needles and basins and plastic bags filled with solutions. There were a few interns ministering to the patients, an older man who looked like a head doctor, and a few student nurses.

The intern filled out a form for them and told them where the morgue was. They took the elevator to the basement and walked down a long hall. There were fewer people here and halls were silent and sinister.

At the end of the hall was the morgue room. There was a wooden double door with no windows, signs that said ABSOLUTELY NO UNAUTHORIZED PERSONNEL BEYOND THIS POINT. On the door was the same sign with one addition; STAY OUT—THIS MEANS YOU. To the side was a stretcher bearing a human being, over it a white sheet. Blue arms and feet stuck out. The corpse had large toes.

The sheet hadn't covered the head completely, some wisps of gray hair stuck out. Ryker guessed by the shape that it was a man.

A young, pale-faced patrolman stood here, his jacket open a few buttons against the oppresive heat of the hallway. He stood alone, not too sure of himself, probably wishing he was anywhere else.

He looked at them. "You the Homicide boys?"

"Right," Fischetti told him, playing it stone cold tough. "You Patrolman Moretti?"

"That's right, sir. My partner is inside. I came out here. I wanted a smoke. They wouldn't let me smoke in there."

Ryker looked down. No cigarette was in his hand. Fischetti had noticed that already. The patrolman could have smoked inside if he'd wanted to. He was a cop. No snotty intern was going to get in his way. The detectives didn't call his lie. They knew why he'd come out here.

"How long since you've been out of school?" Ryker wanted to know.

"Seven months, sir."

"Where's your partner?"

"Inside with the interns."

"At ease, patrolman. We'll go in and have a look." They pushed open the door and walked down a green painted hall to a swing door with a glass window and through this to a room full of iceboxes and down another hall to the dissection room.

There was a smell of preservative and death in this room. There were slanted stainless steel autopsy tables with sinks at one end, so water could be run across them to wash away blood and bits of flesh into a lip at downward side of the table and to a drain.

A small fan was at work near the windows and an air freshener was filling the room with the scent of pine. It did little to hide the odor of burned and rotting flesh.

There were six interns in the room and three naked bodies on the tables. Ryker wanted the burned body. You could barely tell it was a woman. Her breasts were burned and flattened, one so badly burned it had fused to her chest and could not be lifted. All the hair on the crotch had been burned off and her face was a mask of horror that neither Ryker nor Fischetti wanted to look at directly.

The other patrolman was standing in a corner by a table looking down at his shoes. In this room they would be the safest things to look at.

The two interns at the table were a study in contrast. One was tall, with a balding head of brown hair, rimless glasses, a creased face and a long, thin nose. The other was short, with a great shock of red hair, piercing blue eyes and a wide, brutal mouth. The tag on his blood-specked white jacket said his name was Dr. T. Gerhardi. The other doctor was called Bloominghouse. They both nodded at the detectives, lingering awhile on the droopy-eyed Ryker, who looked like a man who didn't give a damn about life, but might give you a tough time if you tried taking it from him.

The two men identified themselves and asked about the body. Bloominghouse pointed at the cooked corpse. Ryker looked down at it a second time, noticing where the flesh had charred, where it was just tanned dark brown and where it was still off-white.

The face was unrecognizable. Her head was bald, all the hair singed off. Her nose was a twisted thing, the skin burned away and the bone sticking through. The bone giving it a corpse look. The eyes had been burned away and the lids were gone. Her mouth was twisted, partly open to expose once white teeth, now cracked in places, chipped and bright yellow from the flame. Dried blood flecked her face.

Ryker stepped away a minute and looked around the room, listened to the water running and turned back. "You know what she died of?"

"We can't be sure till we check. Could be poison or anything," Bloominghouse answered. "My bet is she died of the fall and attendant shock, then the flames ate her."

"How do you know it's a fall?" Ryker asked.

"The X-rays show many broken bones. We've had jump or fall cases before with similar breakage. The cranial bones were pretty well smashed. Massive internal hemorrhage, particularly inside the cranial cavity, would account for death."

"So you think she fell or was pushed into the chimney?"

"I can't say where she fell. It may have been the chimney, it may have been someplace else before she was thrown into the chimney. It's your job to guess that."

"Yeah, it's my job and I guess the chimney. I can't see this woman being dragged someplace, thrown off, picked up and taken into this building, up to the roof, then tossed in the chimney. The guy who did this was logical.

"If he wanted to destroy the body he would put it into the furnace in the basement, unless he was afraid he'd be seen. So he would take her to the roof and throw her down the chimney. If she was dead he would have to drag her up fourteen flights, then one more to the roof, then up all those platforms. He wouldn't take her by elevator. Someone might get on. That's as good as calling the police and telling them where the corpse is. So if she was dead he would have had to drag her up all those stairs.

"Too tough a job. Not something a smart guy like this would do. He would take her up there alive, make her climb those platforms, then push her into the chimney and go on his merry way.

"Was there any sign of sexual molestation?"

"I doubt we would know," the doctor replied. "The fires destroyed the lining inside her vagina. There would be little if any evidence of sexual intercourse. It could be from relations she had with her husband."

"Husband?"

"Yes." He went to a side table and picked up a blackened wedding band. "This was so deeply imbedded in the burned flesh it wasn't noticed till the X-rays. The technician pointed it out on the plate."

Fischetti took out a white bandanna. "Put it here. We'll be needing that." The intern put it on the bandanna. Fischetti folded it up and put it in the breast pocket of his jacket.

"All right," Ryker said, "I guess that's it then. There doesn't seem to be more. No bullet wounds, stab wounds?"

"None. But we'll look. We're about to cut her open. If you'd care to stay—"

Ryker interrupted. "No, thanks. I haven't eaten dinner yet."

The interns looked at each other and laughed. Ryker turned to Fischetti. "Come on. Time for us to be moseying along. We've seen all we need to see here."

Chapter Three

Michael Marlin lit a cigarette as he looked over the evening edition of the *Daily News*. There was nothing so far about a body found in a furnace. There would be when they cleaned it out, if the bones hadn't turned into ash and been dumped by then. He'd got rid of a body that way in Queens six years ago. It had never been discovered or reported. He'd burned that one in a trash dump.

He put the paper down. Nothing to read anyway. Nothing but news about slobs who couldn't make ends meet and the rising cost of living. He didn't give a damn about that, not when he got twenty grand a hit and there were plenty of broads to hit.

Marlin was a specialist, a rare bird, an expert in a field full of experts. He was a hit man, a gun for hire, a rod with experience. In the Old West they called them gunfighters. That was when you had to face your enemy on an open street and he had half a chance of hitting you. Most weren't good, so they died. On occasion a gunfighter did bite the dust, but not too often. Today you didn't have to face your opponent on an open street. You stalked him when he didn't know and when you struck it was swift and savage and, more often than not, from behind. There were the cops, but they were easy to elude. You were free, an agent with a gun and an urge for easy dough.

There were as many varieties of customers as there were hitmen. Hit men come in all ages and sizes. Tough boys with a screw missing, men who were without morals. There are mob hit men, and a more deadly variety who belong to no one.

Michael Marlin was a special kind of boy. He killed only women—wives, to be exact. There are husbands eager to shed their mates so they can be replaced by new women. Divorces are often too costly—stocks, bonds, bank accounts are in names that might keep them. For twenty thousand there was a solution—quick, clean and permanent. The husband just paid the cash, the rest was his job. When he was done the men played the part of grieving husband to the hilt, waited a few months and married. Someone might ask, "Isn't it a bit soon for Joe to marry?" But that was all he'd ever hear of it.

But for Marlin each hit was a memory, one that did not grow with time. He killed, he knew why he killed and he didn't regret it.

He rose from his bed, went to the window and looked

down on Ninth Avenue. The seedy residence hotel was giving him the creeps, but it provided anonymity. It was a place where men saw nothing and asked no questions. The people in it, the management, and Marlin all liked it that way.

He took a last puff of his cigarette. A tug was moving up the Hudson. He looked back at his room. It was getting to him. It would be better to go out. The city was alive at night. Maybe a movie would be best, something with action, a kung fu picture. A few franks, some buttered popcorn, a visit to Nathan's. He would come back tired, satisfied and hit the sack without any worries. There was the twenty thousand tomorrow. Money to go on living.

Grabbing his coat he stepped out, locked his door and went down the threadbare hall to the elevator. A sleazy looking blonde came up the hall. He had seen her here a few times. She looked at him and smiled. He didn't know much about her, but guessed she was one of those nomadic go-go dancers who travel the New York, Boston, Chicago Milwaukee circuit.

It was dangerous to know people. They ask questions and pry and that can hurt. But to live within a shell, to be a hermit, can hurt more. Soon he would remove the mask of anonymity. He would say hello and move in, before someone else picked the apple off the tree. He sensed she was lonely like him, and the last few times had been sizing him up to see if he was someone she could know without being pawed over and jumped on right away. She didn't mind giving sex, which was what he mainly wanted, but he also wanted some companionship and a smile in return. She had sized him up, studied his face, decided he was a nice guy.

Boy, is she wrong, he thought with a smile as he pressed the elevator button and looked down the hall.

Edward Marcel didn't eat supper that night. He didn't call Sylvie, his girl. He didn't answer the phone when it rang. He just sat there numb, horrified and yet relieved, as if a great weight had been taken from his shoulders.

He was trying to think of what to say when the police came to question him. He was sure he had it all down pat now. There would be surprise, but not too much. Shock, loss of function, but not too much. He was nervous and felt the act would go over better with a sense of realism.

He lit another cigarette, went to the window, pulled aside the wine colored drapes and looked down at the long, wide street below.

Ryker and Fischetti returned to the station house, waved to Bo Lindly, who was going out on a call and went to Fischetti's office.

They made themselves comfortable and began talking. Fischetti guessed the killer had wanted the body destroyed, but had failed. When this hit the papers he might be frightened off from more killings.

"I'm thinking about that poor woman," Ryker said. "It was a horrible way to go. I'll bet she didn't even have time to make peace with God. It was up, over and down the chimney."

"Yeah," Fischetti said. "But you've been a homicide dick more than a few years, Joe. There's worse ways to go, though I'll admit this was pretty bad. So far we have nothing to go on, unless you want to question people in the office building."

"I don't have to, Sal. Walters and Donahue are doing that. They have the home addresses of the people who work there and are paying calls now. Still it would be better to wait till tomorrow. This'll hold. It won't rot."

"Sometimes cases do. The killer might strike again."

"That's on the assumption he's a mass killer, Sal. I've found that isn't always the case. Sometimes it can be a love kill. He loves her but he hates her, then he kills her and feels sorry afterwards. A lot it helps the corpse. So he comes and gives up at the station. Nine months later he is taken out of the Tombs, sent before a judge. Some freak nut doctor comes in and says his mother wasn't nice to him. They put him in the criminal nut ward. Some idiot nut doctor sees him twenty or thirty times, then says the guy is sane and lets him out. Three months later he murders another broad. It plays like a record. There are at least ten cases in any year."

"You made one mistake," Fischetti said.

"What was that?"

"No head doctor would say he was as normal as the day he was born and release him. According to psychiatrists we're raging maniacs when we're born. We have to move into the mainstream of society as we develop, which is called adjusting. Those who do not for various reasons are called maladjusted."

"Thank you, Doctor. Now what the hell do we do now?"

"Oh, we can sit here and do nothing. Maybe talk about old times."

"I don't want to talk about old times, Sal. I'm tired. I had a hard day. I go home to eat and you call me back here. I was going to watch TV tonight."

"Forget TV. There's a job to do."

"If you want me to do it, give me facts. I can't walk blind. There are eight million slobs out there." Ryker extended his hand in a wide sweep. "In addition, at least a million others are visiting this city at any time. I can't stop them all. You have to give me clues, so I can narrow the number of suspects down to a more manageable list."

"Don't be sarcastic, Joe. Clues will be coming in, but you have to wait."

"Fine. I'll go home till then."

"Suppose they start coming in?"

"Call me in the morning, Sal." Ryker got up and walked out of Fischetti's office.

Chapter Four

Somewhat satisfied, Marlin stepped from the theater and looked up and down the bright street full of humanity. He wasn't much of a man for films or anything else. Movies rarely left him feeling more than mildly relaxed, a condition that did not last for more than an hour after he left the theater. He rarely went to see the new, high priced movies. It had always been his nature to seek out the sleazy, out of the way places, with the grade B and C pictures, where others of his kind and habit came to kill a few hours in a tawdry life.

For him the movie was the form of relaxation between jobs. He was a man of all hours. He killed when the killing was best. His hunting ground was the United States, the area he knew best. He was cool or hot, cruel or kind, as the job required. He knew his trade well and had fashioned his approach and methods over dozens of kills in the years behind him.

It wasn't just money that made him kill, but the kind of life he had. Michael Marlin was a freak of a very special kind. It was kill or perish. He had no skill, and could not see himself as a shoe clerk at the feet of some fat woman, helping her try on ten pairs of shoes before she bought one for three dollars.

Money had become meaningless over the years. It was just dough. You needed dough to travel, to eat, for broads. Everything was dough. When you traveled, you went by car from city to city. You went through cars and had to buy new ones. You became hot and had to stay out of circulation, and while you stayed out you needed money.

Marlin paid no taxes, had no way to explain his income and style of living if picked up. His life was a closed book. His driving license, plates, identity were false, purchased from a syndicate in Detroit. He often had to change identities, an expensive process, but one his profession demanded.

Even his name, the one he admitted to those few who had got to know him over the years, was false. It was not Marlin but Marlitz. He had lived in Kitchener, Ontario and come into the States illegally in his early twenties to find work when employment was bad in Canada.

He visited Kitchener twice, once when his father passed away and the second time when his mother was ill and sent for him. They knew about his illegal entry into the U.S. and disapproved, but said little as long as he made money and wasn't a burden to them or his two sisters.

Marlitz became Marlin. The immigrant from Germany now became an American in every sense of the word. He worked at losing the thin accent which could give him away. In the beginning people would mention it to him. He would explain by saying he came from the farm country to Minnesota, where many German speaking Americans live. It was a plausible tale and they believed him.

Tired of petty jobs and low pay he traveled to Milwaukee and worked in a brewery. He fell in with two young workers, unmarried like himself, and they palled around together.

One day Eddie Stonehaus suggested they rob the brewery payroll and head to Chicago. The others thought he was nuts, but the payroll came to seventy thousand, a hefty sum. Marlin threw in with Stonehaus and then Krakowski came in and together they planned the job. One day they walked into the payroll office, caps pulled down over their heads, handkerchiefs over their faces. They had everyone lie down on the floor while they took the money.

One of the office girls wore such a short dress it was hiked up to her behind when she lay down. Marlin pointed her out to Stonehaus and whispered a suggestion in his ear. They would take her along and rape her, then leave her on some lonely country lane.

Things did not go well for the bandit trio. Two company guards who were supposed to be in the office were not there because their car had a flat. Instead of the robbers walking in, disarming them and tying them up, they walked in on the robbers.

There was a shootout. Stonehaus and Krakowski died and the two guards were killed, but Marlin came out without a scratch. He discovered his coolness under fire and was able to drop both guards before they could turn their guns on him. His friends had missed, so they died. He didn't miss.

Marlin had stepped over the threshold of lawlessness that day. He picked up the satchel of money, took the girl along to drive the getaway car. He took her into the country, raped her, threw her out and drove away.

A few miles on he found a farmer fixing a flat. Being a good citizen, Marlin got out to help him. When the flat had been changed, Marlin ripped out the wiring in his own car, showed the farmer his gun and took the farmer's car.

He went fifteen miles more, found a lady driving a car and forced her off the road onto a shoulder. Abandoning his car, he made her drive him into a wood where he spent several hours raping her and resting. He tied her to a tree and drove away.

In a few hours he was in Chicago. There, he used some of the connections Stonehaus had mentioned. They took his seventy thousand in hot money and exchanged it for thirty thousand in good cash.

He paid a thousand for a place to hide out, with meals, and once in a while a tired hooker to service him. It wasn't a bad place. They even let regular customers in that hotel. It fronted on Lake Michigan, and on nice days he would sit by the window staring at the blue lake, wishing he could be swimming in it, instead of being cooped up inside.

When the heat was off he left and got a room in a nicer hotel near the Loop. He had been there barely two days when the desk called his room. A gentleman wanted to see him. Curious but wary, he told them to send him up.

The man wore a big homburg and a camel hair coat. He had thick jowls and a permanent blue tint to his face. He was smoking a big cigar and sat down on Marlin's unmade bed.

"You're a new boy in town," the man said. "You and two guys did a job on a Milwaukee brewery. They're dead, but you shot your way out. Now you're thirty grand richer.

"You're good with a gun, a real pro, I hear. Where'd you learn?"

"Nowhere. Just came naturally, I guess."

The fat man smiled. "Oh, a child prodigy. Good. There are uses for a pro gun in this town. A lot of people need heavy iron. You lookin' to hire out? That thirty won't last forever."

The fat man looked around. "Before you know it you'll be wanting to move to a nicer hotel. Then you'll be wanting a car and dames. Them babes cost. Buy me this, that and the other. Take me here, honey, take me there, honey." He laughed and Marlin laughed with him, still confused, unsure of what to say.

He was only nineteen then. Chicago was a big town. The fat man looked him up and down. "My name is Arnold Steinmitz. I work for Danny Arborello. Know him?"

"No."

The fat man grinned. "You wouldn't. You're an out of town boy. Danny is big around here. Only if you work for Danny, call him Mr. Arborello.

"There's two hundred a week in it for you. Take it. You'll be glad. Your troubles will be over." It was 1947, the war was over, unemployment across the land. He nodded. The fat man got up and shook his hand.

"You won't be sorry." He gave him a fancy engraved card with a Michigan Avenue address. "Be there tomorrow, nine sharp."

Marlin stood by the window, looking at the card and thinking about the new life the robbery had opened up for him. He wasn't a punk anymore, but a pro gunman, part of a big time mob.

He went to see Danny Arborello. Danny liked him and hired him immediately. At two hundred a week he became his bodyguard. The girls around Arborello and his men were flashy and cheap.

In early 1948, Arborello was ready to move Marlin up in the world. He asked him to rub out a loan shark. Marlin was given the details about where to find his fish and sent looking. He did a nice job, though he was almost shot in the leg.

His reputation in the mob rose. Arborello was killed by a hit man from a rival mob in July of that year and Marlin thought it was all over. He hurriedly left for his hotel room after hearing the news and prepared to pack.

A knock came at his door. Gun in hand, he pulled the door open and jumped to the wall behind it. Arnold Steinmitz was calling again.

He smiled at the white-faced kid and said, "Put it down. There's been a change in the wind. Danny stepped on some big toes. Now he's gone, but you shouldn't worry. People like you. There's always a place for a good gun." The big man smiled, his blue jowls dark in the shaded room. Marlin sat down to listen.

Ace Riley, boss of the rackets on the North Side, needed a good man. He wanted Marlin. Unsure, Marlin went along and soon found himself in a new scene.

He learned the fine art of garroting from a Swede who worked for Ace. Unlike Arborello, Ace liked to be called by his first name. Marlin did a number of hits that improved his technique over those months.

His salary increased till he was making four hundred weekly, driving a brand new Olds and seeing a torcher by the name of Hannah Brady. 1949 came and went and the list of hits under his belt grew till he was the second most dangerous hit man on the North Side. The police CID squad had already built up a thick dossier on him. At times he found himself tailed by unmarked cars. The boys taught him to double back and go down side streets, speed up and slip away from his tail just as the light changed. He found himself being followed less and for shorter distances.

In 1951 Fats Malone got killed in a South Side bar. Marlin was now the deadliest and most feared gunman on the North Side. He was ready to help Ace move in on the rival mob. They had four or five gunmen even deadlier than Marlin. A bit nervous, he threw in with Ace. Steinmitz heard about it, and one night before Marlin was to go see Hannah Brady, Steinmitz called at his hotel.

He was carrying a briefcase full of money. Steinmitz threw it on the chair and said, "There's fifteen thousand dollars there in tens. The boys on the South Side like you. They also hate Ace Riley. Know what I mean?"

Marlin played it dumb. Steinmitz bent forward till his fat belly stopped him. "Kill Ace. You're his top boy. Get him. The money is yours. Get him and leave town. His people will be looking for you. Go to another city. You'll be safe. Just go."

"Suppose I stay with Ace?"

Steinmitz smiled. "Then there will be two contracts out—one for him, one for you. We can get him. Make no mistake about it. It's tougher without you, tougher going against you and him both. But we can do it. Our way, things get done cheap and quick. Are you game?"

"I don't know, I've got to think about it, Steinmitz."

"This ain't a time for thinking. This is a time for acting. It's times like this that separate the boys from the men."

"Or the suckers from the sharpies."

"You saying we're playing you for a sucker?"

"Could be, Steinmitz, could be. You get me to do the hit, then you wait for his people to hit me. You get two hits for the price of one."

"Don't get us wrong, Mike. I said leave town. That's it. No more worries. Trust me. I haven't steered you wrong."

"There's always a first time. Only in this line your first is your last. I don't want to get up to bat only to strike out."

The fat man smiled. He glanced at the money. "You want a guarantee?"

"Right. I kill Ace, I kill my meal ticket. You know my line. Where do I work after this? I'm not going to quit and become a salesman," he said with a wan smile.

"No trouble. You want work, we got plenty of work. As much as you can handle. I'll se Frank Zucco. He can get you contracts in L.A. Are you willing?"

Marlin hesitated. "Let me think for an hour. Leave a number. I'll call." Steinmitz frowned.

"All right, Mike. But don't delay. This is very important." As he rose to go, he looked at the satchel full of money. "I'll leave this here in case you want to count it," he added with a smile, and was gone.

Marlin didn't have to think long. He called Steinmitz, made the deal, got his instructions and an appointment with Frank Zucco.

Frank was a lined fellow with iron-gray hair and a wide, toothy smile. He had lunch with Marlin and gave him the names of three contacts in L.A.

"When you goin' to hit Ace?"

"In the next few days," Marlin answered. "I have to make sure he doesn't have anyone with him when I hit him. Too many guns can create dangerous flack. A guy can get killed that way."

Zucco, who had been a hired gun in his younger days, laughed. "You're tellin' me. I used to be in your line. You're not talkin' to a dummy. I know how the boots fit. I used to wear them."

Marlin spent the next two days with his pals. It was not till the second day, when Ace Riley had to visit a girl friend and needed a bodyguard along, that he and Marlin were alone together. Marlin did not delay. He stopped the car by the curb on a dead block and looked at Ace, who stared curiously at his bodyguard and chief hit man.

"What's the idea, Mike? This isn't where Iris lives."

"I know, Ace, but this is where you get off." Ace stared in bewilderment, then saw the gun in his hand. He knew now. There had been a sellout, a common thing in the Chicago underworld.

"You were a nice boss. Goodbye, Ace." Three shots from the silenced pistol lashed out at his body. The man fell dead, staining the car seats with dark splotches of red, staining Marlin too.

Marlin drove to a quiet street, parked the car, left the key in the ignition and walked away. On the main thoroughfare he found a cab. The driver seemed shocked at the splotches of blood on his passenger's pants and jacket. He even rose up in his seat to look back.

"Don't be so curious, my friend," Marlin said, offering a fifty-dollar bill. The cab driver was a wise man. He took the money, started the cab and for the whole trip did not look back. Marlin had him stop four blocks from the hotel.

He went in the back way, took the service elevator and once in his room called Zucco. The man was very pleased. There was a one way ticket to L.A. waiting in an envelope for Marlin.

"Get out of town today," Zucco said. "Long guns will be looking for you. His mob is wrecked, a chicken without a head. They'll be easy to pick off, but a few will get away. They always do and those will be the ones who can get you.

"Don't say goodbye to nobody. Pack just what you can carry, pay your hotel bill and scram. Two of my boys will go with you. They'll wait outside. When you come out with your suitcase, they drive you to the airport. Got me?"

"Sure do," Marlin answered. He was curious about Zucco, feared a doublecross. The boys sent along to help him might really be out to kill him.

Wary, he packed and checked out. When he got into their car, for the ride to the airport he had three guns—one in a shoulder holster, one in his waistband, and one in an ankle holster.

He insisted on riding in the back with them up front, and got his way. They drove him to the airport, wished him well in L.A. and even shook his hand. Relieved, he got on the plane and sat back for the ride, suspicious of a bomb in the baggage.

The ride was uneventful except for a brief thunderstorm over the Rockies, and they were winging their way over the desert and across the broad, sunny expanse of Los Angeles.

He checked in at a moderately priced hotel and after a few days touring the city went and bought himself a car. Then he went calling on the people Frank Zucco had mentioned. Two of them were mob, the third was an independent named Bertram Himmelweiss, a German immigrant like Marlin. Without exposing his identity, Marlin befriended Himmelweiss and went to work for him.

Himmelweiss was a specialist. He contacted people who wanted jobs done. He checked them out to make sure they had money, were stable and not police fronts. Then he assigned a hit man. The hit man talked with the client, stated his fee, got relevant details and began to tail his victim prior to the hit.

Like any good agent, Himmelweiss got ten per cent. Marlin murdered actors, dancers, hookers, store owners, wives of rich insurance agency heads. It was here that he got into the wife killing business and it became his specialty.

By 1953 the police were getting scent of him. It was time to take a vacation. He went to Reno and stayed in a hotel near a popular bar—known as Diane's Dive. He came there frequently, sometimes to meet divorcées, who are as common in that burg as pigeons in Central Park. At times young fluff congregated and he would try to score with them, but they were just looking for rich suckers so they could have a good time for the ass they gave.

Marlin had money, he wasn't bad looking and he was young, so he had no trouble meeting fluff. It didn't cost him half the money to have a good time that it would cost some old guy.

Eventually Marlin got to meet Diane. They struck it off fine and he spent many sunny days escorting her around town.

But Reno wasn't the world. Marlin's money was beginning to run out. Work called. The heat was off in the big town. He bid Diane a good time, said he would call soon, though they both knew it was goodbye forever, and then he left.

Himmelweiss had branched out. He was not only getting contracts in L.A., but in San Diego, small towns in the San Fernando Valley, upstate as far as Frisco. Life was good for his hit men.

Marlin's closest scrape with the law and death came when he was doing a hit in Frisco. He had knocked out his victim, an attractive redhead, put her in a car and drove to the top of one of the innumerable hills. Just as he let out the hand brake so the car could plummet down the hill and carry the woman to her death, a cop car came on the scene.

They saw the car, saw Marlin and tried to go up the hill. The woman was coming down in the car, so they could not go up. One of the cops jumped out of the car, while the other drove down a side street, to come up the hill from another direction.

Marlin was already in his car and moving. He went down the other side of the hill fast. He knew without thinking that a bulletin was now out on him and knew the cost of being caught was the gas chamber at San Quentin.

Leaving the scene at a hundred miles an hour, he outran three cop cars, made it to the North Shore district he knew well and skimmed through alleys, along the garbage lined waterfront, down narrow side streets full of kids playing stickball. Marlin didn't care if he hit anyone, and small bodies flew through the air. There is no killer like a desperate one.

He was able to elude his pursuers, get out of the city into the wide country. That evening, in another car, newly stolen, Marlin picked up his hit money, ditched his car and got a flight south to L.A.

It was one of his deadlier days and for the first time he was nervous. He did not do another hit in Frisco for two years after that.

Himmelweiss heard about his close call and had Marlin come to his spacious, oak paneled office near Culver City. When the gunman entered, Himmelweiss rose and shook his hand warmly.

Marlin knew the approach was bull. Himmelweiss was the coldest fish he had ever met. His informant network extended throughout southern California. There was little he did not know or hear.

Himmelweiss wasn't always around. At times, his junior partner, a man named Manny Frishenwasser, held down the office. When Himmelweiss wasn't in he was out talking with contacts or clients or over in his girl's place near Beverly Hills. She used to be a B-grade actress, but now serviced a small, well-paying clientele. A nice girl to know if you had money.

"I hear you're having trouble, Mike," Himmelweiss said with a hint of accent.

"Had trouble. But only once. No more." He lit a

cigarette and exhaled quickly.

"But you had trouble." He looked up coyly, like a blushing debutante, then down again. "That's not good. You could have been seen. Someone tells the cops. They get a description. They circulate a drawing. They wait, watch, listen. A contract gets handed out, then boom, you get caught. Your cover is blown, so is ours."

"No, it isn't. I'm good, really good. They won't catch me."

Himmelweiss sat back in the chair. "A lot of the boys tell me that. Then they go out and get caught. You can't play with the odds. I like you, Mike. You're good with a gun, good with your head, good planning a job, but you're a liability now."

Himmelweiss put his arms out as if to be crucified, and shrugged. "What you gonna tell these cops when they catch you? What you gonna say you been doin' all these years for a livin'? Where you live? Who your friends are? You got nothing to say. They'll take you in and keep you there.

"All they've got to do is pin one job on you. It'll all over then. The only decent thing is that the gas chamber isn't as painful or messy as hanging. You got to get out of town. This place is too hot for you, Mike."

"Is this a dismissal?"

"No, Mike. Just a transfer from one place to another. You go to New Orleans. It's a nice town. A sunny place on the Gulf, fine fishing, and nice women, I hear. Never been there myself."

"I don't fish. What's for me on the Gulf?"

"More hits, Mike. We don't forget a guy like you. You're top people, and top people don't get screwed. There's a boy we got there. An associate by the name of Gold Coast Ciccone. They call him Jimmy. Don't be shy. Go see him. We'll call ahead."

"Here you're in a kettle of fish. There you're a free man. Ciccone owns a firm, goes under the heading of Brandywine Industries. Everything circulates around that."

Marlin wasn't too pleased, but on second thought, it was better than staying here waiting to be snowed under. L.A. and Frisco were tough towns, with a lot of cops who would rather shoot first and ask questions later.

He hung his head. "As long as I'm going, I'll go today. No use waiting."

"Good man. I knew you'd understand." Himmelweiss got up and came around the desk. He put an arm around Marlin's shoulder and added, "I'm going to put in an extra good word for you. Jimmy Ciccone will love you and them Louisiana boys are well bought. Not much trouble from the police there if you're in the Mob."

Marlin remembered that as he went home to pack. In no time he was on a plane to New Orleans, non-stop. Five hours later he got off, looked around at the bright landscape and went for a taxi that would take him to a hotel.

He stayed in one of the better places and spent the day in his room, watching TV, listening to the radio, reading the local papers to get acquainted with the new atmosphere. You had to feel at home, or you were dead.

At five in the afternoon he dialed the number he had been given and asked for Wilbur. "No Wilbur here," a disembodied voice answered. "This is the Gilbert Tobacco Shop."

"Then let me speak to Wilbur Gilbert of the Gilbert Tobacco Shop." There was a pause on the other end. He had said the right words in the right order.

"Who is this, please?"

"The name is Marlin. Who's this?"

"Mr. Marlin." The voice was pleasant now. "We have

been waiting for your call. Rather late, isn't it?"

"I was in no hurry. I didn't think you would be going anyplace." The voice chuckled and asked where he was. Marlin told him the hotel and room number.

"A man will be over shortly. Don't leave your room."

"I'll be waiting," Marlin said. There was just a click as the phone was hung up at the other end.

Another fat man came to see him. He laid down the law about the way Jimmy Ciccone ran hits in this town.

"You no kill anyone in a church. You no kill anyone in front of his loved ones or a school. You no—" the fat man went on and on. Marlin knew the code of ethics, if you could call it that.

He sat up. "When do I meet the people who will give me jobs, and how much do they pay?"

"You're a quick man, Meester Mike."

"In this business you are either quick or dead." The fat man laughed and nodded his agreement, squeezing the fat folds of his neck together.

"So you not a time waster. Jimmy will be glad to hear that. He likes a man that moves, and so do I." For the first time since he had arrived the fat man held out his hand, and Marlin shook it.

"I am Vito Martessa, his uncle. You and I will be friends." Being a friend to this old man was a joke, but Marlin smiled. This was where his money lay, so he smiled deeply.

"You can do your first hit in a week. We want you to case the area well beforehand."

"No need to worry about that, Vito. I always case a place well. Leave it to me. How much do you pay for a hit."

"Twenty-five hundred. That includes expenses. Whatever you spend, you take out of that sum." Vita stopped when he saw the look on Marlin's face. "What's the matter? Not enough?"

Marlin shook his head. "In L.A., I got five g's for a hit. I was one of the best. You must know my Chicago background."

Martessa smiled again, but the phony old-country charm wasn't working, so he dropped it. "We know all about you, Marlin."

"For that kind of money, I don't work. I'm not small league any more. You want a good boy, you have to pay good prices. I'm fair, but I'm no sucker. I didn't come off the boat yesterday."

Martessa looked at him with hot, black eyes, that narrowed. "You lend me a nickel?"

"Sure." Marlin fished one out of his pocket. Martessa went to the door and turned to look back. "I return in a minute."

Marlin heard him walk down the hall to a pay phone. When the party answered he spoke in Italian for a minute then hung up.

He walked back to Marlin's door. "I talked to Jimmy. He says okay, but you better be good. He don't pay too many guys five g's. He wants his money's worth."

Marlin waved his palm in the air. "Don't worry. With me, everyone gets their money's worth. Now tell me about this guy I'm supposed to hit. Or is it a broad? Lately I've been specializing in wives."

Martessa smiled. "This I don't hear. Tell me." So Marlin did. A week later he had his first hit, a rich funeral director, and five thousand in the bank.

By 1955 there was no better hit man in New Orleans. Marlin liked the area, the fishing in the Gulf, for which he was getting a taste, and the tarts.

He was friendly with a torcher by the name of Ellen

Vartana. They were lovers till she was killed one night in a car accident on a rainy side road near Bayou Peche Rouge.

Marlin was tough. He got over it in no time and went looking for another girl, but none seemed to satisfy him as she had. He dated infrequently thereafter, preferring the finer houses in the French Quarter. It cost him, but he had the money.

The wife killings in Frisco and L.A. had attracted the attention of the F.B.I. They came into the case in 1955, when the local police reached a dead end, and followed a trail strewn by bits of news informants gave out.

Posters began to appear in the post offices offering five thousand dollars for the whereabouts of three different men. These were the top guns in the Himmelweiss group. There were no photos, just descriptions.

Then one day Himmelweiss was killed by the boy friend of a woman he was seeing, who had at least three others on the side.

The police who checked through his remains found a thinly coded black book. In it were names that could be deciphered, with dates and initials next to them. The names of hits and the dates were compared. They matched. The initials of the hitmen were not coded when they had been jotted down in a hurry.

The F.B.I. had a foot in the door. They went looking for Manny Frishenwasser. He was arrested, booked on a series of charges including possession of stolen firearms. They found two of his gunmen and arrested them. The first murder they pinned on the youngest gunman. He faced the chamber and still refused to talk. He feared the mob even more than the chamber.

The testimony of these men wasn't essential, but their back trail was. Through it the F.B.I. found many of the people they had dealt with, known, or gone out with.

Through persuasion, promises of immunity and anonymity, they got damaging testimony. Three more hit men were picked up, one fled and was caught in Reno.

Strippers, call girls, petty con artists told about other hitmen, big guns from the east, who had come to L.A. to practice and then left. Some resembled the descriptions of the three men on the post office sheets.

A name came up, Mike Quinone. This was the one they wanted most, the one with dozens of hits, whom they tracked back to Chicago and before that to Milwaukee. They suspected he may have crossed the border. People reported that when he was angry or excited, which wasn't often, he retreated into a thin, reedy accent, German-sounding.

He claimed to have come from the Minnesota mining or farm country. The story had so many variations the F.B.I. discounted it. They were almost positive he came from Canada.

Meanwhile, they followed the missing hit men, aware the entire country was caught up with the news about Murder, Inc. Here was a more sinister and less well-known organization. Who was Mike Quinone? No one knew. In Reno, women came forward who had known him. Someone told about a woman named Diane and the place she called Diane's Dive, and the tall, dark man she had been living with years back. The F.B.I. visited, questioned, probed, cajoled and got what they wanted, but all it did was lead back to L.A.

Then luck broke for them. There was a major hit in New Orleans. Marlin rubbed out Tony Marrone, numbers king of the waterfront. Tony had grown too big for his britches, the boys decided, so Mike Marlin was picked to put him in a smaller set. He did the job and vanished into the night.

This time witnesses reported to the police. The F.B.I

checked, and noted the close resemblance between the killer and the man they wanted. Their New Orleans office got cracking. A dozen special agents arrived from Washington.

Within three days an informer called Jimmy Ciccone. Scared blue, he called Marlin up to his office, which was over a big night club in the French Quarter. It was a wide, airy place with floor-to-ceiling windows, a wide balcony and nice iron work.

Jimmy was a short, wide-shouldered man, with thinning black hair plastered on his skull, a wide, brutal mouth and plenty of gold teeth that shone when he spoke, making even a little grin appear a large smile. It masked his true intent and fooled many who have known better.

"You called and I came, Jimmy. What's up?"

Jimmy rose from behind his oak desk and walked around it. "We got trouble, Mike. I mean, you got trouble," he emphasized, pointing to Marlin. "But your trouble can become mine. This is no good. I'm worried, so I call you."

Marlin waited, not saying anything, letting the other man put his cards on the table. "The F.B.I. is lookin' for you, fella," Ciccone told him after a pause. "Gold Coast Ciccone can't get involved."

He looked Marlin straight in the eye. "You're hot goods. They catch you, they pin you on me. They say I hired you to kill people, which is true. Worms come out of the woodwork to say it's true. Not so far, but take my word, they will. It's always like that. When you ridin' high, everybody like your behind. When you down they all put on their Sunday shoes and come around to kick you in the ribs.

"You go to the chair if they get you. They'll fry you, Marlin. Me," he thumped his chest with a hairy hand, "I get the same treatment. We're one of the few groups that have stayed out of their clutches so long, and they hate it.

"In New York, they took Lepke and put him on the hot seat in Sing Sing. He don't say a word about us. He keep the oath of silence until the end. Then the guard pull the switch and it's all over. His worries are gone, but mine have just started. I don't want to die that way. So get your ass out of here. Go far from here. We give you ten grand living expenses. Stay low till it cools off. Then you come back."

"But how long?" Marlin asked. Jimmy shook his shoulders. He didn't know.

"Three, six months, I can't say. I'll give you ten grand cash. That should be enough."

"Suppose it isn't?"

Jimmy looked at him. "It should be. Don't spend like a hog. Stay someplace where you don't get noticed. When it runs out dip into your till. You've been making good dough since you came here."

"Wait a minute, Jimmy. I don't splurge. There are times when I spend, but not always. I don't have money enough to last me. You'll have to send me more if the ten runs out."

"I'll give you fifteen. No more. Don't try to bargain with me. I won't let myself be pushed. Now take the dough and get out fast."

Marlin nodded as Jimmy counted out the fifteen thousand in fifty-dollar bills. "Don't even call me for six months. This has got to blow over. You have no idea how smart these F.B.I. people are. You ever deal with them?" He stopped and answered his own question. "Of course not. If you had, you wouldn't be so calm. I couldn't hold you here. Wild whores couldn't hold you."

"Thanks for everything," Marlin said as he pocketed the cash. As he walked away, Jimmy thought, that's three hits you owe me. Nobody takes fifteen g's from Gold Coast

Ciccone and does nothing for them.

Marlin went straight to his hotel, packed his stuff, checked out, put it into his Cadillac and drove away. He did not go to the airport, figuring the cops might be checking all passengers. They wouldn't check the roads, not unless they set up a roadblock, and none had been set up.

He drove east toward Florida, sleeping in motels, eating in cheap joints and half-decent restaurants. He got a chance to see the country, wasn't impressed and drove on. By his calculation life didn't mean much anyway, now.

Taking his time, Marlin worked his way down to Miami. It was an easy, pressure-free life, not one filled with waiting in the car, casing the victim, planning the kill, then closing in and the gut wrenching chase away, sometimes followed by cops, witnessed by passersby.

Marlin began to enjoy himself. In Miami he got a room in a nice hotel, lolled by the swimming pool, ate good meals, chatted with people who were decent, straight, normal, not gangsters. For the first time in years he got a look at a different world.

What he saw made him think about his youth, when he had been innocent. The last eight years began to seem like a bad dream, apart from the real life that should have been his.

But the straight world was for those who fit into it. If he went straight it would mean doing work suited to his level of skill, a beer factory hand, taxi driver, small time trucker. No, for Michael Marlin there was but one road, the one he was on.

When he thought of the five thousand he got for a hit and how long the people around him had to work for that kind of dough, he smiled. They weren't better than him, only lower. They were patsies, making it the hard way. Marlin was smart.

That day he went looking for Tony DeTorio, close friend and partner of LaRue Guiteau, a Cajun who had gone bad, joined the mob and was here now, operating fishing boats by day, illegal book on the dog races by night.

DeTorio was the kind of partner you could hate down to your roots. He was tall, thin as a reed, with dark skin, black hair, long sideburns and the face of a Cajun. He wasn't, and that was another of his deceptive features.

In public he talked like a pillar of society. In private he was cold, foul-mouthed, and crude. Marlin learned to dislike him fast.

When he first met him, DeTorio was lifting crates filled with ice and lobsters from the back of his station wagon before bringing them into the restaurant he and Guiteau used as a front and headquarters. It was called the Aces High. The sign was a fly-specked, whitewashed wooden board over the entrance with the name painted in what had once been bright purple.

Marlin followed him in and asked for Guiteau. DeTorio put a crate down on a small table and turned around in the hot, dim atmosphere of the restaurant.

"What do you want with LaRue?" There was a trace of Cajun accent in his voice, probably not real. Like the rest of his act, it was an acquired habit set up for a purpose. If DeTorio did it, it was not for nothing.

"I've got a message for him."

"From who?" DeTorio was a hot blooded character who could hold it in, but only for so long. Marlin's answer would count.

"Gold Coast." DeTorio grew less wary. His body began to relax, but not too fast, while he thought it over. Finally he extended a gnarled hand, then picked up his crate and carried it back through some swing doors to the kitchen. Marlin waited.

A dark-eyed girl appeared from the kitchen. She had a knife scar running from under her eye all the way down her left cheek. She was barefoot.

When DeTorio came out, he pointed to her and laughed. He had a nice way of laughing that made him look almost decent, but that was deceptive.

"Our second cook," he said. "Calls herself Isabella. Who knows what the hell her name is? But she comes to work on time, makes a decent meal and is good under the sheets. Want her?"

"I'll think about it," Marlin answered.

"She's a crazy, scarfaced bitch-killer. Be careful with her. She'll carve initials in your ass with her blade."

DeTorio smiled at her. "Show it to him, Isabella." The girl smiled in a demented way and pulled out a wooden-handled blade about six inches long, then put it back into a scabbard between her breasts. A nice chick, Marlin thought.

Marlin looked around the restaurant. There was a framed motto on one wall, high up where everyone could read it. The sign said: "Violence Begets Violence." That was probably for the drunks.

DeTorio went out of the restaurant to bring the other crates in. Marlin looked back. Isabella had gone inside again. DeTorio came back, gave him a beer from the dark mahogany bar on the right side of the room and went to sit with him.

"I called LaRue. He'll be here soon. So you're one of Jimmy's boys? I haven't seen Jimmy in a year. What do you do for him?"

"Repairs."

DeTorio snorted and smiled. "Can't talk, huh? That means you must be a big boy, on the lam from the law. An assassin, maybe?"

He bent from the waist, leaning over the table and

smiling. Marlin took a sip of beer. Not his brand, too warm, tasted like piss. He wondered how much business this place did.

"Tell me, mister. You got all your teeth?"

DeTorio gave a wide, toothy grin, as if to let him see his teeth. They looked bone white in his face.

"You mean to tell me you never had to make an emergency visit to the dentist to have your teeth rearranged?"

"No, I like them where they are."

"If you like them where they are," Marlin said, "learn not to ask questions of strangers. Because I'll let you in on a secret. Tooth decay is not the major cause of dental problems."

DeTorio smiled less now. He had seen something in the eyes across from his. He knew enough to keep his big mouth shut and wait for LaRue to arrive and take the flack. He rose. "Finish up your beer, sir. I'll be going now."

"Of course. It was charming meeting you." Then Marlin looked back down at his glass and DeTorio went away silently.

LaRue Guiteau did not arrive till half an hour later. Marlin had been sitting in the dark, playing with his empty glass, making wet circles on the check tablecloth.

Guiteau was a short man, like many mobsters Marlin had known, with cold eyes, a hawk-nosed face and long ears. He wore a green knit shirt open at the neck.

He sat across from Marlin. "Who are you?"

"The name's Mike Marlin. I knew Gold Coast in Orleans. He spoke of you often. I came looking for work."

"I got all the kitchen help I need, Mr. Marlin. No work here."

"That isn't the work I'm asking for, and you know it. I was one of Ciccone's top hands. Ask him if you don't believe me."

"He ain't here, Marlin. He's a thousand miles away."

"You got a phone," Marlin answered coldly. Guiteau rose and said he would be back in a short while, then disappeared through a door to the left of the table. Marlin saw a dim, carpeted office beyond and sat back to wait.

Time passed and Guiteau returned. "Ciccone talked to me personal. He gave me the general drift." There was respect in his voice. He had heard about Marlin. This was no ordinary hoodlum, this was a pro killer.

"Ciccone doesn't want you circulating yet. The F.B.I. is nosing around."

"Oh, I thought that was over."

"I guess not," Guiteau replied. "There's more. They picked up scents here and there. The F.B.I. is moving its investigation down to Florida. Someone told them about you. Ciccone says stay put. No move, nothing. Besides, you're a hired gun. I don't have that many rubout characters to give a man like you. I understand you come high—five thousand a job."

"That's right. My money has been drifting away and no work coming in. This is a nice stretch of country, but I'm getting sick and tired of sitting around doing nothing."

Marlin fished a cigarette out of his jacket and lit up. He blew smoke across the table and fanned it away with his hand. "So's that's the setup as of now?"

"That's it, Mr. Marlin. The only employment I could give you would be to speed up payments from those who are a little slow in coming up with gambling debts. You know how these things are done."

"I've learned along the way."

"But all I could pay would be three hundred a week—not much to a man in your income category. And I'd have to ask Gold Coast for permission. This would put you back in circulation in a prominent way, more than being a hit man. He pointed to himself. "I'm the one who will suffer if you're caught. Your neck is my neck and the balls you lose may not be your own.

"Understand my side. Thinking about it, even if Ciccone said it was all right for you to come in with me, I would say no. If you ask elsewhere, they'll find out about you. In the end, you'll get no work here or elsewhere.

"Take my advice. Lay low. Kill time as best you can, and wait. This will blow over. It has to. Those fools can't keep it up forever."

Marlin nodded, bid Guiteau farewell and left. He returned to his hotel, checked out and went north. Time for him was a never-ending road. He wound up in Tampa.

The weeks and months that followed were spent drinking away the hours in dark bars with pink lights and lonely ladies looking for new suckers to replace the ones who had gone away.

They were months spent eating alone in hotel dining rooms and roadside joints, riding the same highways, lounging by pools, along the beach, getting a dark tan, visiting the track, drinking too much on occasion, smoking till his lungs felt like lead, gambling in back rooms with sleazy characters.

Bit by bit his money dwindled on room and board, for gas and repairs, clothes and cigarettes and drinks. Money went away on women and games of chance, and none was coming in.

At the end of summer he returned to Miami, tired, tanned, looking healthy but sick inside. Marlin was getting fat and soft, he was no longer what he had been. He went back to the Aces High, where Guiteau and DeTorio were. The place looked unchanged, as if waiting for him to come home.

The F.B.I. had given up the trail and Guiteau greeted him warmly. Ciccone still did not want him in New Orleans, but Guiteau wanted him here. For three-fifty a week he would be his enforcer, a new occupation for a pro like Marlin. Once in a while he would shoot a debutante or a rich widow.

The months passed in a blur of beatings, killings, hot tropical nights, pasty, scared faces, ugly sneers, laughter, booze, dirty money paid in back rooms.

In April 1957 the police raided the back room of Aces High. They found a unique card game going. The men were arrested and booked. In subsequent lineups witnesses identified men in that game. There was a trial and despite attempts to buy the witnesses, jury and judge and even an attempted rubout, DeTorio, Guiteau and Marlin got three-to-five.

For Marlin it was his first acquaintance with jail. The confinement without women, comfort or drink, the menial labor and set hours jolted him. But it wasn't forever, so he bided his time. In prison, he made the acquaintance of several other mobsters. They had their own club and if you were in it they never quite treated you like the others. For money you could get sent to solitary, and there hookers came to you. There were catered meals from the prison kitchen, booze and cigarettes. Prison, when you had connections, money and crooked guards, wasn't such a damn bad place after all.

In October 1961 Marlin got out on a year and a half parole and cooled his heels in Tampa, waiting out the time so he could get going. He waited for Guiteau and DeTorio to come out. They had drawn stiffer sentences than he had.

He wanted to throw in with them, and also to throw in with Ciccone again. In 1962 the others came out and together they decided to set up a heroin smuggling racket that would work through the Keys and up along the Florida Gulf Coast.

Taking their cargo off small boats in secluded coves and narrow beaches, driving through the grassy Everglades across the Tamiami Trail and into Miami, they had a good thing going.

It lasted eight months. The F.B.I. came in, broke it up, arrested DeTorio and Guiteau. They didn't get Marlin. They set up roadblocks, an all points bulletin, but he drove night and day till he made it up to Tallahassee and hid out in a drop joint. It cost him for this sanctuary, two thousand but it was worth it. He stayed there a week and then with new plates and a repainted car began his drive to New Orleans. Only Gold Coast Ciccone could save his ass now.

Gold Coast was older and somewhat more philosophical when Marlin returned. He was surprised that Marlin wanted his job back. He knew all about his former gunman's recent past and how versatile he had become in the years since he had left New Orleans.

"You want your job back, Mike, huh?"

"That's what I said."

"You changed, Mike. You lookin' older, sorta tired."

"Not that tired that I can't case a kill and pull a trigger. What about the job, old timer?"

"I ain't such an old timer. If you want the job, sure. But I got to caution you, it don't come cheap no more. The cops are out hard on a gunman's ass. They caught Two-Fingers Abolardo in Dallas last summer, drilled the top of his skull off. Those police play rough and hard. Most of the mobs have their own people, regulars, who do hits once in awhile."

"I know how it is. My ears are open."

Ciccone fingered his jaw. "I could use you. How much you figure on gettin' for a job, five thousand?"

Marlin laughed out loud, more of a snort than a laugh. "Where have you been, Gold Coast? Ten thousand is the pay for a hit nowadays."

"Not always. You hear what that fink Valachi says on TV. They paid him twelve hundred for a hit, one hit. Not much to kill a man. Only a day's work. Twelve hundred."

"That was ten years ago, and it was a small hit. Today he gets at least twenty-five. I hear there is a fifty thousand contract out on him."

"One hundred thousand." Ciccone smiled. "You need dough, why don't you do it? I tell everyone, you collect."

"If you tell everyone, I collect a jail sentence. The F.B.I. will hear. They have long ears."

"I got flunkies to do the killings now. Once in a while you get outside people, they want jobs done. They go through their bookie or loan shark. You know what I mean. Lately we've been gettin' a lot of independent operators. Want me to put you on the list?"

"Yeah, sure. Better than joining a school of flunkies." Marlin went out into the cool night air of the French Quarter.

Two weeks later he got a job to knock off an industrialist's wife in a fashionable suburb. The price was eighty-five hundred. His reputation as a wife killer was stalking him, and it was this which was giving him back his occupation. But jobs like that didn't come often in New Orleans, and many weeks he just cooled his heels. One night he visited Ciccone to say he was going to Florida. There were not enough jobs here. He asked Ciccone to put him in touch with the right names and announce his specialty. Marlin left and in a few days was strolling the streets of Miami.

Work was more plentiful here. Rich men vacationing in the warmth felt the robustness of their youth and sought to replace their first choices in marriages with a second without the attendant costs.

Discreetly, he worked things so that he was doing about one hit every two weeks. He sent presents to DeTorio and Guiteau, now doing time for the dope rap, and checked to find if the F.B.I. was on his trail yet.

They didn't come in till the fall of 1964. He stayed around a few months more, watching his step, then went up to Orlando to cool his heels.

The constant tailing, killing, hiding in dark rooms during the day, coming out to prowl bars and balconies and rooftops at night was getting to him. By now his price had risen to an average ten thousand for each kill, and the suckers gladly paid it. He started to deal directly with the customer, and gave the middleman who connected them ten percent. With the F.B.I. here it was wise to wait.

He rested three months, then took a plane back to Miami. His contact told him the F.B.I. had given up the search and he could start again.

Within two months there were three more dead women, and his trail was again being sniffed by the authorities. They found nothing, but he knew it was time to leave for other parts. With the right contacts and names, he took a plane for Chicago.

He made friends, found women, started a killing spree and soon came to the attention of the Chicago police and when they had trouble getting his scent, the F.B.I. He became known as the Wife Killer. They had a whole file on him in L.A., another in Frisco, a third in Miami. He was getting to be well-known.

Marlin tried going underground, then coming out, doing a few jobs and going back under. Even this way he found that six months was all he could spend in Chicago without getting so hot that his contacts wanted him out. So he left.

He had no friends here. Steinmitz, his old contact, had died of cancer six years before. Time had passed. Sadly, he left for L.A. There were hits to be done, bars to visit, broads to connect with.

What happened in Chicago happened here too. Six months and he was as popular as Billy the Kid. He was a man alone, and he learned to live that way. Marlin took his money, packed his bags and left for New York.

By commuting between New York and Boston, varying his technique, killing men also, he was able to stay in the northeast for over a year before it became too hot and he had to take a plane south.

He decided to stay in Miami a few months. On a visit to the Aces High, he found scarfaced Isabella. She greeted him warmly, gave him a seafood dinner, served him drinks, and pulled the front of her dress open to show him there was no knife concealed there.

She was taking care of the place while DeTorio and Guiteau were in jail. Isabella wanted him to stay with her. She smiled a toothy smile and showed off her girlish charms.

Only she wasn't girlish any more. Time had made her fat and ugly. Marlin did not want her. He knew the saying that the older ones knew what they were doing, but he didn't care. The younger ones needed the practice too.

Marlin made the visit quick. He said he would call when her bosses got out of the slammer and hurriedly left.

He was getting sick of Florida, the dog races and the beaches and the fools with straw hats and the oldsters. He wanted action, but caution told him to lay low.

He left for New Orleans. Here life was a little better. He went to see Ciccone and a few kills were lined up for him. There was no hurry. He could take his time doing them.

The F.B.I. soon learned that the next spate of wife

killings was going on in New Orleans. They came looking for him but Marlin had learned by now that if he was careful he could operate even in hot areas for months without being pinned. The police did not know whom he was going to kill, only he and the one who had hired him and Marlin's contact man knew, and none of them would be talking.

It was summer when he went to Houston. This was new ground for him. Wherever there were men with money who wanted new wives, he knew he could put up shop and find all the customers he could handle.

When the spate of wife killings hit the papers, the police were baffled. Unlike police in the bigger, high-crime cities, they had never dealt with anything like this and it was months before they began to operate efficiently.

Marlin spent eight months in Houston. He liked it. This was a town different from any he had lived in, nicer in a way.

But the law called and he went back east to Philly. He had never done any killing in that town. It would be a new start.

The gangsters were thick in the streets and you had to be quick if you wanted to keep ahead. Marlin had a rep, so that brought him automatic respect from killers, bookies and top mobsters, who ordinarily wouldn't have given him a second look.

There were a number of memorable kills in Philly. He knocked off two mobsters' wives. These days the ladies were getting independent—they wanted divorces themselves, but often an errant wife had information that could hurt her husband.

Killing was the best way and instead of letting the mob do it, which would be frowned upon, they hired him, an outsider, a guy who had done plenty of kills and could be counted on to keep his mouth shut.

One wife died in a cement mixer. He poured her into a foundation mold, and now she was the cornerstone of a downtown office building owned by the mob. Here she would rest for decades, only to be discovered by some wrecking crew well after the turn of the next century.

Another wife was knocked over the head and thrown onto the railroad tracks before an onrushing commuter train. It was a clean kill as far as Marlin was concerned. He got away, and in the end that was all that counted.

Seven months was all he had in Philly before his trail grew hot and the boys told him to take his business elsewhere. He stopped off in New York and Boston for a few hits, then headed up to Buffalo, another town he had never been to.

A local numbers runner was having trouble with some small fry. For ten thousand he wanted Marlin to kill them all. It was half of what he usually took, but it was something to kill the time and he was doing a mob chieftain a favor that would be returned some day.

From here Marlin went south to Miami, where he could take a vacation from his task. In Miami he could find someone to kill the hours with.

He found a woman who owned a bar and restaurant, as many of his women had. She used to be a torcher, she was no longer young, but he wasn't either.

He spent nine months in Miami with his new girlfriend, spending hours in her restaurant, where she sang three nights a week when the piano girl was off. He took her on moonlight drives, spent days at the beach, nights at the dog racing track and nights at her apartment.

As time passed he grew restless and edgy. It was time to go back to work, to replace the money that had gone away like water.

Marlin bid her goodbye and took a plane to Los Angeles. The times were hard, not too many killers needed now. After two months in L.A., he hopped a plane to New York. It was early 1970 now. Marlin was ready to settle into the biggest city in the country and stick around. He had been buying new identities for years and now had another.

Around him the world had not changed. People got up to go to work, worried about money and their jobs. In Marlin's world an entirely different set of ideas ruled. To him inflation and joblessness meant nothing. All that counted was getting the kill and finishing the job.

Chapter Five

Ryker wasn't in a good mood when he got up that morning. He was tired of being called at all hours. Still irritated, he stood in the shower and winced as the cold water splattered him.

He got out of the shower, toweled off and went to make himself breakfast.

Finished eating, he washed his dishes, dressed and locked up the apartment. He got the car from the neighborhood garage and drove to the station. He was sure Fischetti would have the information he wanted.

When he got inside, he waved to the sleepy-eyed desk sergeant and the tired-looking Bo Lindly. He went up the stairs and down the hall to the second floor section that held the Division Homicide Squad room. He went straight to the pebbled glass cubicle occupied by Sal Fischetti. Fischetti indicated the wooden chair in front of his desk and looked down at the report he was reading.

Ryker sat and waited. Fischetti would talk when he wanted to. A fifteen-year veteran of patrol and detective duty, Fischetti knew his job well. Ryker had known him for eight years now.

"Find your way home last night?" Fischetti asked, still without looking up.

"No trouble," Ryker answered, waiting for the other to make his move.

"Bo Lindly will be working with you. Do you mind?"

Ryker shrugged. "Why should I mind? Bo's a nice guy. A little stupid at times. Young, but I got nothing against youth."

Fischetti looked up at Ryker with his clear blue eyes. He threw the report on the desk. "Read it. You need the practice."

Ryker picked it up, skimmed over it quickly, reading with his lips, a habit he had picked up in high school and could not break.

"It says the print reports from the F.B.I. indicate this body is that of Betty M. Marcel, age forty-six, height five-four, eyes brown and so on. Last known place of occupation the Anslow Building near Columbus Circle. Employer Martin Bowenstein of Oelsner Insurance. What kind of a dump is this?"

"He insures cars, homes, small businesses. We haven't called him yet. Her occupation was typist-receptionist."

"You think this boss of hers was running an affair with

her and had her bumped off when she got too pushy, or did the job himself?"

"Could be," Fischetti said. "You'll have to check on that one. Here's his address—442 East Seventy-Eighth."

"What about this Betty Marcel? Have you checked her teeth X-rays?"

"That's being completed. We've found, or rather the people in Washington have gone over to the IRS and looked at her back income tax. You have no idea how much information about themselves people have to spill on tax forms. The way I figure it, she should have filed some sort of medical exemption with signed bills from doctors and dentists. I assume people like that have tooth problems."

"Was she married?" Ryker asked.

"Yes, she filed a separate return. We have a request for her husband's file too. Her husband is two years older than her. His name is Edward Marcel."

"I want his address. We can visit the dude. No use waiting. Maybe he can fill us in on details we might need. You know, marital discords, a jealous lover who kept hanging around and made hubby mad. This lover could have wanted her to divorce hubby and marry him. She wouldn't, because of the financial loss involved," Ryker speculated.

"You know how it goes. A woman gets to that age and wants a change of cock. Something younger, stronger, harder. It sometimes leads to murder."

Ryker tossed the sheet back to Fischetti, who leaned back in his swivel chair, looked at his fingernails and said, "This is going to be a hard one, Joe. I can feel it."

"No, it ain't. It'll end fast. Sometimes the ones you worry about most go the quickest. I'm usually right." Ryker rose to go. "I'm going out to talk to Lindly. You call me when you get anything else important."

"Where will you be, Joe?"

"I'm going down to the corner for coffee. Send someone if you need me fast. Otherwise I'll be back in twenty minutes."

When Ryker came out of Fischetti's cubicle he looked around for Lindly, but didn't see him. From somewhere came the tapping of a typewriter and the sound of a beer can being opened.

Ryker stopped Arch Griswell, one of three black plainclothesmen assigned to this precinct, and asked, "Where's Bo?"

"He went to the Candy store. They been working him too hard. Yesterday, all night and now today. That guy has nerves of steel to take it."

"Cut the shit, Arch. He's young. You did the same when you were his age. Worse, if I remember."

Ryker went down the stairs, across the precinct lobby and out front. A thin wind was coming off the choppy Hudson, sweeping the cold air inland. Ryker pulled his trench coat tighter around his body and set off down the cracked sidewalk towards the candy store around the corner.

The street was lined with the usual assortment—the mugger looking for a target, the stray hooker out early because she didn't make enough the night before.

Ryker didn't pay attention to them. Many knew who he was on sight. They had been around long enough to know most of the plainclothesmen ten blocks away, and if they were new to the area, the others would point out the men you had to watch out for.

The candy store was owned by Rita and Luis Morales. They had owned it fourteen years and were a solid fixture in the neighborhood. Lindly was talking with them when Ryker walked in. They turned to greet him and Lindly also turned to see who was coming in. He nodded and said, "So you come here for coffee, too?"

"You know that, Bo. Don't act surprised." Before saying more he turned to Mrs. Morales. "Let me have a cup of mud, two sugars, well stirred, no cream." Then he turned back to Lindly. "Fischetti says you're on my case."

Lindly slapped his head. "Not you, Ryker, not you."

"Yeah, ever lovin' me." Ryker had known Lindly when he was still a precinct cop. Lindly was now a Detective Sergeant Second Grade. He was younger than Ryker, a tall kid with blonde hair and good looks.

Ryker's coffee arrived. He stirred it and blew on it to cool it faster. "What's the new case?" Lindly wanted to know.

"Haven't they told you yet?" Ryker looked him straight in the eye.

"All I know is that they fished some woman out of a furnace, something like that."

"That something," Ryker answered, "is called Betty Marcel. The F.B.I. did a quick search on her and we are trying to find out pertinent facts about her."

"The only pertinent fact is who murdered her," Lindly answered. "We both know that's all that counts."

"It isn't all that counts, but it's enough, Bo."

Ryker sipped his coffee. They fell silent. When they were finished, they paid Mrs. Morales and returned to the station house. Fischetti was waiting eagerly for them. He had new information.

Chapter Six

The short, fat man, with the bald head fringed with mousy brown hair looked up when Marlin walked into the back room. He indicated that the other two players at the table should get lost.

When they were gone, Marlin sat down and put his arms in the pool of light from the overhead bulb. "How's everything, Poagie?"

Poagie Reeves smiled and took the cigar stub from his mouth. "Not good, not bad. How's tricks in your circle, Mike?"

"The same. I understand you want to talk to me. I got a message from the desk in my hotel saying Poagie wanted to see me. There's only one Poagie I know."

The fat man puffed his cigar. "There's a man named Purcell. Wilbur E. Purcell. Big investment broker on Wall Street. He has a shrew of a wife, showed me her picture. The Hound of the Baskervilles looked good compared to her." Poagie paused, then said, "He wants a hit. Soon. He's tired of her. She interferes with his fun."

"Never mind why," Marlin said. " How much does he want to pay?"

"I told him the price."

"What did he say?"

"Didn't even blink, Mike. He thinks twenty is cheap for putting him out of his misery."

"Did you tell him my terms? Did you tell him we'll have to meet?"

"Yeah, I told him, and he's willing." Poagie ground out his cigar. "Know where the Ryder Theater is, in the west Forties?" Marlin nodded. "Near there is a restaurant, Matilda's Place. Got it? Matilda's Place."

"I heard you the first time, Poagie."

"Just want to make sure you got it right."

"I got it right. Now how do I know who he is?"

"He's wearing a brown suit and a dark blue wool overcoat. He is going to be sitting at a table in back, by himself, drinking hot chocolate. He will be there at eight tonight. You go in, look around, then walk past his table and say, 'Is the hot chocolate good here?' He'll say, 'Reasonably so, try some.' You sit down, you talk turkey, you make a deal and he tells you how to get at his dear wife."

"After he arranges things, you kill her, collect the twenty and pay me ten percent." Poagie smiled widely.

"I do all the work, you do nothing, and you make two thousand. You know how long some slob has to work for two thousand?"

"Now wait a minute, Mike." Poagie raised his arm defensively. "Without me you wouldn't know where to go. I'm the man who directs you."

"Yeah, Poagie, in every town there's one like you. When a guy goes fishing he needs a worm. The same way, I need you." Poagie smiled weakly.

Marlin got up. "You'll be hearing from me."

Edward Marcel paced the floor of his kitchen. He had not gone to work today. He was too distraught. He had taken one of his wife's tranquilizers, but it wasn't working as fast as he'd hoped. The pill was making him sleepy.

He had been waiting for a police call, but none came. Maybe they hadn't found her yet. He was supposed to meet Marlin at two in the afternoon. If Marcel did not show up, Marlin would know he was being detained by the police. Marlin would call to make another appointment.

He had thought of calling the police, but wanted to wait. He should have called by midnight, but didn't. That was an error. It was something a concerned husband would do. He hadn't.

Marcel went to the refrigerator and got a can of beer. He could say he had thought she was staying with her friend Sally, but she called when she did that. He could say he didn't want to be a picky husband, so he didn't call. A weak excuse, but something to say.

It was breakfast time now. The smart thing would be to call Sally and ask if Betty was there, then to try her mother's or wait till her office opened and call there. Then he would call the police and report her missing.

He tried Sally first. Her husband picked up the phone.

"Hello. Who is this?"

"Phil?"

"Yeah?"

"Phil, listen," he let tension into his voice. It wasn't hard, he was tense. "Betty didn't come home last night."

"Let me tell Sally."

"No, wait. I thought she was staying with Sally, like she sometimes does. I didn't want to be calling to check up on her. You know how it is. But it isn't right her not calling to tell me."

"She didn't come here, Eddie," Phil interrupted. There was some incoherent talk off the phone, then Sally came on. "Hello, Eddie?"

"Yeah, it's me, Sal."

"What's this about Betty?" He went through the whole thing again. "You didn't have another spat?"

"No, no. Things are fine, looking up between us. I didn't know. I thought maybe she went to some hotel without informing me. But I didn't think it possible. After all, everything has been patched up between us. I called just on the chance she might be with you."

"No, she didn't come. Check elsewhere. Maybe she's at her mother's."

"Okay, I will." He started to hang up but she held him.

"Eddie, give me a call. I want to know what's what."

"I will. Thanks, and goodbye, Sal." He hung up. He was trembling. Sweat stood out on his forehead and neck. There was a raw feeling at the pit of his stomach. He had laid one set of troubles to rest. Now for the others.

Lindly and Ryker each read the new report that had come in. Betty Marcel had a husband, no children. Her husband was named Edward Marcel. They lived at 311 East 66th Street.

Her husband made over ninety thousand a year, owned a furniture manufacturing business whose advertisements could be seen every other day in the newspapers and on a local TV station.

They would visit Marcel first. That would be the best thing to do. They would also check with the missing persons bureau to find if anyone had called to ask about Betty Marcel, age forty-seven.

Marcel had just finished calling her mother. The old bitch had been alarmed, of course. She wanted to call the police, but he had restrained her, though barely. He had promised to call the office at nine.

He thought she was going to have a heart attack before he hung up, and that brought satisfaction to him. The woman had made life hard for him many times, and it was good to see her suffer.

It was almost nine. He picked up the phone and dialed Betty's office. Milton Weisman came on and said she wasn't in yet. Hadn't she left home on time?

"That's it, Milt, she just didn't come home last night. I thought she had gone to stay with her friend Sally, or maybe her mother."

"That's terrible, Eddie." A note of concern crept into Milt's voice. Maybe he liked the bitch, Marcel thought. If so, he could have made an appointment to see me and I would have sold him all rights to her for five thousand dollars. I was sick of her anyway.

"Shouldn't you call the police?" Milt suggested.

"I will if she doesn't get there in the next fifteen minutes. I'm worried," he answered, again letting a note of concern creep into his voice.

He was sure the police would ask around later and wanted to leave an impression with everyone he spoke with.

"I'll tell the boss," Milt said.

"Good, you do that. I'll wait fifteen minutes and call back."

"I shouldn't be asking this, Eddie, but are you having marital problems?"

"Nothing, Milt. Believe me, things are just fine between Betty and me. There was a time when we were drifting apart, but it was never very serious. Things are just fine now."

"Glad to hear that, Ed. Okay, I'll be going now and if she comes in before you call, I'll tell her to call you."

"Fine, thanks." He hung up and looked at the phone. His knuckles were white on the receiver.

Marlin got up and dressed, went down for breakfast to a store not far from the hotel where he had been staying for the past few weeks.

Breakfast for him was always the same—two rolls, butter, coffee with cream and sugar. He had a leisurely smoke, bought a paper at the corner stand and went back to his room to read. It was his custom to go through the news slowly. He had developed the habit over long years when he had little else to do, because tiny bits of information which might indicate the police were after him could be buried somewhere in back, where he would not notice if he went through the paper quickly.

There had been a jewel robbery at the Hotel Pierre. There had been a new battle in Indochina. An old lady had been mugged and raped by six youths with knives. Hard luck.

Then he came across a two-paragraph item that made him sit up. An unidentified body had been taken from a furnace in a building near Columbus Circle. The building and address were not given. But a number, where the

Homicide Division could be reached, was printed. There was the usual reminder that all names and identities would be kept anonymous. He put the paper down and began to pace the room. So they had found her already. He looked at his watch. He was due to meet Marcel at two.

That fink had better have the money. No, what was it he said? yes, he would go to various banks with Marlin and withdraw funds and Marlin would have to guard it himself, he did not want to have that much money with him overnight. He had even offered Marlin a bank check, but Marlin wasn't that dumb.

There was nothing to do now but wait and hope the guy wasn't a rat. Though in all his years no one had ever finked Marlin. Hit men rarely get cheated. If they do, it's usually no more than once.

Marcel put down the phone. He had just finished calling his wife's office. The boss himself had answered the phone and sounded concerned. He told Marcel what a fool he had been not to call the police last night. Marcel said he would call them right after he hung up.

Even doing that wasn't so easy. He had to get the Missing Persons Bureau. They had to find the number and give it to him. When he finally got the bureau, they sent him from desk to desk till he got the man he needed.

The sleepy-voiced clerk was explaining that he would take the missing party's name, age, description and address, last known place of employment and so on. He explained the bureau didn't start looking for anyone till they were missing for at least twenty-four hours, sometimes longer.

"Missing wives are pretty common these days. Don't be surprised if in a short while she comes back sorry."

"Look, mister, I know my wife. She wouldn't do something like this. There has to be a reason. Maybe she's been kidnapped."

The man on the other end laughed. "Many husbands imagine that. What really happens is that their wife has been kidnapped by a romantic notion. Don't worry, she'll be back."

"Easy for you to say, it isn't your wife. Just tell me when they'll start looking."

"When did you first notice her missing?"

"I expected her home about six last night. When she didn't come I thought she was staying with a friend, but she wasn't. I called the place where she works and she wasn't there, either. I called her friend and her mother, then I called you. I checked."

"That means we can't officially start to look till six tonight. But the office doesn't work then, only a small emergency crew. We'll start tomorrow, bright and early."

"What the hell do you mean, tomorrow?" Marcel hoped his explosion sounded good. The man tried to calm him.

"I know you're angry, but try to understand my side. I don't make the rules, I just follow them. I'd like to help, but I'm a cog in a machine."

"Okay, mister. You don't have to cover. I understand. Just take down my report. If I have any beef, I'm sure I can speak to a supervisor."

"Look now, mister, don't blame me."

"I'm not," Marcel interrupted. "You're just a poor slob working a job. I'll talk to those who can do something. I'm not a poor man. I own a firm. I have money, connections. I'll do something."

"Good luck, sir," the clerk answered. "A lot of people talk that way. They just have no idea how large this bureaucracy is. However, you're welcome to try."

"I'll have to have your name, your wife's name, your occupation and hers, age, characteristics, identifying marks, funds available, so we can check bank accounts."

Marcel went through his name and address, her name and address, her weight and age, the whole process. After several minutes, including repeating the same thing over so the clerk could catch it, he was done.

"Thank you, Mr. Marcel. You'll be hearing from us."

"When?"

"If not in two days, give us a call. We tend to forget things because we deal with so many people. When you call us, you give us a jolt and that gets us going."

"I'll do that," Marcel said before hanging up. What a bunch of idiots, he thought. If he really had to depend on them to find her he would never get anywhere.

Ryker drove and Lindly sat beside him. Fischetti had suggested they go up to see Marcel first.

They walked through the marble lobby and were stopped by the doorman, who was chatting with a guy mopping down the floor. They showed him their badges and went on their way.

The doorman and janitor looked after them and speculated whom they were going to see. Ryker hadn't told them, all he did was show his badge and say he had business in the building. The doorman was so awed by the detective that he said okay and let them go on.

The two men got off the elevator and walked down the carpeted hallway as Ryker commented, "Just look at this. Wall-to-wall carpeting in the halls. In my building the only thing we got wall-to-wall is roaches."

When they first entered the building, Lindly had cast a quick glance at the register and noted Marcel's floor and apartment number. Now, they found it and rang the bell.

When the bell rang, he almost jumped, but he calmed himself and wondered who it was. It couldn't be the police.

They wouldn't come till the Missing Persons Bureau struck out, and they had not yet begun looking.

He opened the door and barely stopped himself from gasping. The two men who stood there could be nothing else. The older one, with the droopy eyes and the hard face, looked dangerous.

From the past, the two detectives knew people were generally nervous in front of them. Many even knew what they were from a mile off. They tried to handle the person easy at first, even if they suspected him.

"May we come in?" Lindly asked. The man nodded dumbly and stepped inside. He pointed to a long hallway carpeted in brown with nice furniture and crystal chandeliers.

Mr. Marcel was a man of moderate height. Not too fat, nice features, well groomed. Not the kind that looked like a womanizer or a drinker.

He brought them into his foyer. They could see a kitchen beyond and breakfast things on the table, set for one. He sat them down at a large, dark mahogany table and asked if they wanted refreshments.

When they waved aside his offer of coffee, they got down to particulars. "We've come about your wife," Bo Lindly told him frankly.

Surprised that they had found out so quickly, Marcel wondered what kind of a fool he had hired to do the hit, and then if his own neck would be in danger once this fool was caught.

Shock showed in his face as he sat with wide open eyes and mouth. They took his surprise as an indication that he was afraid something had happened to his wife.

There was nothing they could do. He would have to be told, and to add to his horror, he would have to go down and try to identify that mass of burned flesh.

There is no nice way to tell someone his beloved is gone, so you do it fast and hope for the best. At least that's the way Bo Lindly looked at it.

They sat and watched him sink back into his seat. "What are you saying, gentlemen?" He was looking at Ryker as he asked this. Ryker suddenly realized they had come in without identifying themselves as detectives or showing their badges, and that Marcel hadn't even asked for identification.

"You wife is dead, Mr. Marcel," Ryker said. His face was cold. Marcel didn't break down or cry. He sat upright, stiff, a frown creasing his brow.

The next thing he said was, "I guess I'll have to call the Missing Persons Bureau and tell them not to bother."

"What do you mean?" Lindly questioned.

"When I saw my wife didn't come home, I was worried. I thought she was staying with her friend Sally, or her mother. I don't want to seem like I'm checking up on her, so I didn't call. But this morning I called Sally. She said Betty wasn't there. I called Betty's mother and she wasn't at her mother's, so I called her job and she hadn't arrived yet. She should've been in by then. So I called the police. They connected me with Missing Persons and they took all the information.

"But now you tell me she's dead. I guess the rest doesn't matter." He fell silent. The detectives looked at each other. Lindly asked if Marcel minded if they smoked. He shook his head and in a minute both of them had lit cigarettes.

They asked about her job, their relationship, if she had been staying away from home much lately. All the answers were moderate. Not too much trouble. Her job was okay, she liked it. She had been staying away from home some lately, but not too much.

"Mind if we look in her room?" Lindly asked, rising as if

permission had already been granted. It was a little trick he used. If he was already up it would be harder for someone to refuse.

Marcel shrugged, confused, wondering what they could find. He rose and went ahead to the bedroom, down a short hall to the left.

The bedroom, like the rest of the apartment, was done in dark, traditional furniture, with wall-to-wall brown carpeting on the floors, framed pictures, mostly prints.

The detectives probed here and there. On her dressing table they found lots of cosmetics and some tranquilizers.

Lindly looked at Marcel. "Your wife have nerve problems?"

"Mild, the usual stuff. Not too bad. I wouldn't classify her as suffering from a nerve problem, no sir."

They fell silent and searched on. He stood, hands in pockets, a bit worried, but content that there was no evidence of foul play. After all, he had not done the killing, a professional had. Some deep confidence told him he was safe and out of the woods.

How long they stayed there he did not know, but it seemed like forever. He didn't want to look at his watch. A distraught husband doesn't do that. Someone with something to hide does.

They stopped abruptly, after putting some of her garments back into a drawer rather neatly. Marcel had always thought cops were messy. These two looked like goons, but weren't.

"Let's go back into the foyer, Mr. Marcel," Ryker said.

As they went Marcel realized he had not asked how his wife died, where they had found her or the rest of the details.

"Wait," he said. "I've been in such a state I haven't asked how she died or where you found her."

"That's right, you haven't," Ryker said, looking back. Marcel flinched. The man spoke each word like an accusation.

"How do you even know it's my wife?" Marcel asked.

Ryker shook his head as they sat down around the table. "We're sure. We have her print reports and her teeth X-rays should soon be identified by her dentist. If you could give us his name and address it would simplify matters."

"Sure, sure," Marcel answered, confused by the quick rush of events. "She went to Dr. Arnold Melnick over on East Sixty-Eighth. I forget the exact address," he said irritably. "You can look in the phone book."

"That we can," Ryker answered. He was beginning to get on Marcel's nerves. He was too damn cool about things.

Lindly was writing down what Marcel was saying and it made him nervous to have each word taken down.

Then Ryker turned and said, "Have you ever had any indication she was seeing another man?"

Again Marcel showed shock, not knowing what to say. "Wait a minute there, Mister. Don't be trying to pin that on my Betty. She was a good wife, a damn good wife, the best a man could ask for. There was nothing between her and anyone. Nothing. We were happily married. She loved me, I loved her. We had a good sex life."

Marcel fell silent and stared moodily down. The two detectives looked at each other, then jotted more notes. The sound of their pens going across the crisp white paper was driving him mad.

"How did she die?" he wanted to know. "Where did they kill her? Who did it?" The words came out in a mad jumble.

"We found her a few buildings from where she worked. Someone had taken her up on the roof." Ryker paused.

Marcel looked up, his eyes wild. He licked his lips. "You

mean they raped her?" he asked almost shyly.

Ryker shook his head. "No, they didn't rape her. I didn't get a report to that effect, thought it may have occured.

"We don't know who did it. It had to be a man, because," he paused, "because they lifted her up and threw her down a chimney into a furnace. She was probably killed by the fall before the flames got to her."

Though he had paid for the hit he was jolted at its brutality, and hid his face in his hands. A sob escaped him. He kept this position for about a minute then looked up. The detectives sat like stone, as if they hadn't moved all the while he had his hands over his face.

"That must have been horrible," Marcel said, thinking that he would wish a death like that on no one.

"Murder isn't pleasant, Mr. Marcel," Ryker said. "However, it's our job. Now, are you sure there's no boy friend somewhere in this?"

Marcel shook his head. "No, not at all. My wife was loyal to me, very loyal."

"You mean there wasn't the slightest hint of suspicion in your mind?" Lindly questioned. Marcel shook his head.

Lindly looked at Ryker, then the two got up. "All right, Mr. Marcel. We'll be going now. I don't think there's anything else to ask."

"What about my wife's body? I'd like to view the remains."

The detectives looked at each other. Sure, why not, they thought, they didn't have much to do now. They'd take him to the morgue at Bellevue.

Ryker helped Marcel get his coat on while Lindly held the door.

Chapter Seven

Marlin was walking back to his room from the elevator, when he noticed the sleazy blonde fiddling with her key.

As he walked by he asked, "Having trouble with the lock?"

She cast him a sly smile. "Yes, perhaps you can help."

Turning so he faced her, Marlin smiled graciously and said, "My pleasure." Close up, she smelled of cheap lilac perfume. She had a narrow, full-lipped mouth, almond-shaped eyes outlined by black mascara, pink frost lipstick, a thin layer of powder and a bedroom look to her face.

Perfect as a time-killer.

He got the door open and extended his hand inward, as if welcoming her into his own apartment. She went by him, letting him get a good look down the front of her dress and then gave him an upward glance as she asked, "Won't you come in awhile?"

He jiggled her keys on his finger, smiled and followed her. He closed the door and stood there looking around. It was a bigger apartment than his, two rooms and a bathroom.

She pointed to a faded little couch near the unmade bed and said, "Sit down, please." Marlin sat with his hands on his knees like a shy suitor and waited.

"Like anything to drink?" she asked, showing him a half-full bottle of bourbon and some dixie cups.

"Yes, I'd like some, not too much." She smiled, turned back and poured him a cup.

He took it, sipped and said it was all right. She waved a hand around the room and said, "It's too damn small, this place. But when you're on the road, what can you expect?"

"On the road?"

"I'm a go-go dancer," she said. Then looking down at her figure, she added, "A nude go-go dancer in one of those bars over near Forty-second street." She smiled coyly. He had known from the beginning what she was. You can smell these sluts from a mile away. Marlin didn't care, so long as he got something.

"It sounds like an interesting job."

"Shit, it ain't really." She sat down next to him. "I have to dance long hours and I sometimes get so tired. Then there are all these creeps that try to paw me. The bouncer has to take care of them."

"Every job has its good and bad points," Marlin answered.

"That's true," she said between sips. "But this job has more bad than good. I guess that's the way it is in this racket. You spend a few weeks in a town, then move on to something else."

"It sounds kind of lonely," Marlin answered.

"Not always," she smiled. "Sometimes you meet friends on the way."

"Like me?"

She looked down at her bourbon, then up at him. "What do you do for a living?"

"You wouldn't believe it. I sell industrial insurance."

"Who to?"

"Industries, of course."

She began to laugh. "How silly of me. I wasn't thinking. Somehow I can't imagine you as an insurance salesman."

"Would you like to see one of my policies?" he asked with a smile.

She shook her head. Her intent was not for him to show her his policies, but for her to show him her talents. He waited, leaving the next gambit to her.

"Have you ever been to the Purple Panther?"

"No, I don't think so."

"You sure now?" He shook his head. "You go to any nude go-go places?"

"I haven't had a chance yet. I've seen a few movies so far."

She smiled. "The dirty films?"

"I'll see a few this week. So far I've only seen some of the regular ones. A Kung Fu film or two, some westerns, you know those terrible Italian westerns."

"I know. But you haven't seen any nude go-go dancers?"

"Not so far."

She smiled. "I've got to do something about that. You haven't been over to the Purple Panther to see me, so why don't I give you a demonstration?"

"Why don't you?" he echoed her. She smiled, went to a small stand in the corner and put a record on one of those cheap portable record players you can buy around Times Square.

Acid rock came from it and she turned down the volume. She fiddled with her zipper in back, pulled it all the way open and then her dress slid down. She stepped out of it and threw it on the bed. She was wearing only sequined bikini briefs, pasties and a smile.

The window was open and bright light filtered in. She came closer to him, swaying in time with the music, going faster and faster. Then she slowed down and began to remove the pasties. She rubbed each nipple after she took off the pasties.

She looked back at him and said, "We don't need those. After all, I'm not at the Pink Panther and the house rules don't require wearing pasties."

"Do they require wearing briefs?" he asked, sitting forward, his mouth wide open.

She smiled, shook her head and began to remove the briefs. She stepped out of these, threw them to the side and continued dancing.

Marlin finished his drink in one gulp and put it down, then watched her dance faster and faster, the beat of the music building and her dancing becoming more frantic, sweat pouring out of her and him too, as he watched her dance.

As the dancing reached a crescendo, she dropped onto his lap. He looked surprised, but only for a moment. Their lips met in a kiss that went on and on and on.

Chapter Eight

Ryker and Lindly brought Marcel back home. He was a broken man after seeing what was left of his wife. They asked if he needed a sedative, and he told them no. He had friends who would look after him.

When they left Marcel, Ryker and Lindly stopped at a deli for lunch, then drove back to the precinct to see if there was anything new. There wasn't.

They drove up to the Columbus Circle area to visit Martin Bowenstein of Oelsner Insurance, Betty Marcel's former employer. They wanted to know something about her relations in the office, any important events that might have occurred on the day she died.

The detectives found parking, then took the elevator up to her office. Ryker stopped a woman at a desk in front, showed her his badge and asked to see Mr. Bowenstein. She nodded, showing confusion and pointed to a medium-sized office at the back inside a wood and glass cubicle cut in two by a partition.

The woman went ahead of the two detectives, asked them to wait, then walked the last few feet to the office on the left. Ryker noticed that the talking around them had stopped. She knocked on the door, the man inside looked up from his work, motioned with his hand and sat back.

The two detectives walked in past the woman, who closed the door behind them. Ryker had a good chance to study Mr. Bowenstein. He was in his early sixties, with straight, snowy white hair, combed back along his skull, a long nose and thin mouth, and pale blue eyes with crows' feet. The skin on his face was pulled tight as if by constant tension. He looked like a tough customer, the kind who had come up by pulling at his own bootstraps.

"We're detectives, Mr. Bowenstein," Ryker said, flashing his badge. Bowenstein glanced at it briefly, then looked out at the main office. The typing and working picked up again. Bowenstein looked to his left and nodded to the man in the other office. He rose, came out of his office, opened the door to the one the three men were in and stepped inside. He was shorter than his partner, thick in the middle, with a bald head and a fringe of bright brown hair. It looked unreal to Ryker, who decided it was dyed.

The other man was introduced as Leonard Beiman. He was smoking a thick cigar and Bowenstein didn't like the way it was stinking up the office. After a few seconds he said, "Hey, Len, put out the damn cigar. It's stinking up the office and giving these guys a headache."

Beiman put out the cigar in the ashtray on Bowenstein's desk, then moved to his partner's side. "What is this about, gentlemen?" Bowenstein spoke with a hint of accent.

"Betty Marcel has been murdered." Ryker watched for reaction on the two faces.

"That's terrible," Bowenstein said. "How did this happen?"

Ryker gave him a quick rundown, touching most of the bases including her husband's reaction. Bowenstein shook his head gravely, wisely.

"A sad thing. I don't suppose you know who did it. If you did, you wouldn't be here."

"That's about the size of it," Ryker told him. Bowenstein cast a glance at Lindly, who wasn't talking.

"Well, all I can tell you is that I wasn't in the building when she left. I went home about four. I do that some days, other days I stay till six or eight, depending on the work load. I just went home early that day."

"However, ask Len." He nodded at his partner. "Len had her stay to type up some things. She stayed late, didn't she, Len?"

"Yeah, I had her stay. In fact, I was the last to leave before she did. She told me she had an hour's work yet. I said I'd put her on overtime. It was so important, I said I'd give her double time if she stayed and she said she would."

He looked at his partner. "You don't mind I offered her double time, do you, Art?" The other shrugged. It was too late to argue about it. It was something that would not happen again. It was money owed to a dead woman, and probably never to be collected. Marcel wouldn't be thinking about her wages now.

The questions Len was asking Bowenstein showed who was the real boss, and who was the minor boss. Ryker wanted to know what happened next.

"Well, I had to go, so I told her to lock up the office. She's very reliable, I mean, she was very reliable, and she'd done it a few times before. She locked up the office nice. She put the cover over her typewriter. Everything was in order."

Lindly looked at Ryker and said, "That means the killer must have got her outside the office, maybe down in the street."

Ryker nodded agreement. "Who went to lunch with her that day?" He was looking at Bowenstein when he said this.

Bowenstein scratched his forehead, then he closed his eyes in remembrance. When he opened them, he said, "It was Cora Jamison. Go call Cora," he told Len. "Tell her these two gentlemen want to speak to her about something."

Len went and got Cora, a woman about Betty's age, but blonde, slim, with a nice smile and gracious presence. Looking at Bowenstein, Ryker wondered how she had managed to keep happy in this place.

He asked about her friendship with Betty Marcel, learned that it went as far as the office and no further, and that she was about as friendly with the other men and women in the office.

"Did she seem different yesterday than on other days, as if she had some worry?"

"No, she didn't, Sergeant." Cora shook her head, sending her hair flying. She pushed it to the side of her head and continued. "Everything was the way it had always been. Nothing seemed to be different."

"She had no worries?" Ryker wanted to know.

"Not that I know of, or that she told me."

Ryker reflected then shook his head up and down. He smiled before dismissing her. "Thank you, that's all, Miss

Jamison."

"It's Mrs." she smiled back.

"Then thank you, Mrs. Jamison."

As she walked out, he turned back to the partners. "You have anything to add? Anything you saw indicated? Any worry out of the ordinary? Come clean with me. I know you don't want to get involved, no one wants to these days. But if we find out you held back we'll really be on your behind. Think now. Anything you remember, we can use."

The partners thought, then shrugged at almost the same time. Ryker and Lindly bid the two men goodbye and added that they might drop by tomorrow.

When they went down in the car Lindly asked Ryker's opinion of all this. "I can't say. Could be they don't know a thing, or they know some minor stuff they think may be important and isn't. They'll hide it from us just in case they might get involved.

"What do you say we go up and look over that roof where she was killed, though I doubt we'll get anything more now that the forensic boys have been through the place."

"Fine by me, Joe." It was a gray, sooty place, as they noticed. Thin twine with red lettered police signs urging the public to keep out were in evidence around the platform where the chimneys were located.

The two detectives climbed up to the level of the chimneys, and looked around at the city below. "Beautiful view," Lindly commented.

"I guess so," Ryker answered absentmindedly, as he examined the area for evidence of a struggle. There would be none, not on concrete and brick. There would be little or nothing new to find, that he was almost sure.

He still looked, though. The old habits of a homicide dick die hard. He and Lindly took turns staring down into the hellish maw of the chimney till they could see no farther in the blackness. Each tried to imagine the horror of Betty Marcel as she was shoved down this thing.

The killer couldn't have carried her, unless he had the strength of an ape. He probably held a gun on her and forced her up on the platform, then knocked her out and forced her down. Or maybe he was a sadist and just shoved her in. Lindly shivered as the thought struck him.

Ryker stood straight and looked around. "Nothing more for us here. We'd best be going now, Bo. Get back to headquarters and discuss this with Fischetti. He should have something to tell us now. At least I hope so."

Chapter Nine

Marlin dressed, fixed his tie and looked at his gold wrist watch. He was late for the appointment with Marcel. Oh, well, there wasn't a customer yet who minded having to wait before he paid his money.

Casting a glance at the sleeping, nude form of Lilly Barron, as his go-go girl liked to call herself, he smiled and then walked out of the darkened room and down the hall to the elevator.

Marcel looked at the wall clock for the fifth time. He

© Lorillard 1975

C'mon

Come for the filter.   You'll stay for the taste.

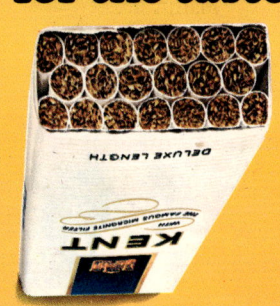

19 mg. "tar," 1.2 mg. nicotine av. per cigarette, FTC Report Apr. '75.

Warning: The Surgeon General Has Determined That Cigarette Smoking Is Dangerous to Your Health.

© Lorillard 1975

I'd heard enough to make me decide one of two things: quit or smoke True.

I smoke True.
**The low tar, low nicotine cigarette.
Think about it.**

King Regular: 11 mg. "tar", 0.6 mg. nicotine,
King Menthol: 12 mg. "tar", 0.7 mg. nicotine, 100's
Regular: 13 mg. "tar", 0.7 mg. nicotine, 100's Menthol: 13 mg.
"tar", 0.8 mg. nicotine, av. per cigarette, FTC Report April '75.

Warning: The Surgeon General Has Determined That Cigarette Smoking Is Dangerous to Your Health.

was here as Marlin instructed, but Marlin hadn't showed up. Maybe something had happened. For a man who had already gone through so much since morning, this was the worst part. He hadn't called Sally yet, or Betty's mother. If he did, they would be all over him and he couldn't get away to pay Marlin.

Since a little after two, the phone had rung three times. He had picked it up and listened without answering. Each time, an excited famale voice had said, "Hello, hello?" Marcel had hung up.

He was sure one of those calls was from her mother. He had had enough of Betty's mother and would have no more of her if he could help it.

He went to the bedroom and lay down. He looked at the bed she had slept in, and would not sleep in again. He would have to sell this stuff and buy a new bedroom set before he married Sylvie. He couldn't bear to bring her here with the memory of his former wife floating around in the background.

He was thinking of Sylvie, thinking of calling her, when the phone rang. He hesitated. Was it Betty's mother, or Marlin? He lifted the phone and listened.

"Hello, hello. Ed Marcel?" It was Marlin.

"Yeah, hi. How's tricks?"

"How come you didn't answer right away?"

"I thought it was my wife's mother. I'd have to tell her about Betty and she'd be over here in a shot and I couldn't go with you."

"They found her?" Without waiting for an answer he said, "Tell me about it." Marcel gave him a swift rundown.

"So that's how it was. What do you expect when you put a stiff down a chimney? She burns, she smokes, the attendant comes running, stokes the furnace and sees the body. Still, it's better than throwing her off the roof, which

I was going to do till I saw the chimney and got the idea. I was going to shoot her, but changed my mind. You know how these things go."

"How did she die?" Marcel asked, horrified and fascinated at the same time.

"I never talk about hits. I did one time and the guy felt awful. He was puking for a week. You want someone dead, but you don't imagine it happening. Believe me, it's better that way. Now get dressed and meet me in front of your building. I'll be carrying an attache case. I've come prepared."

The phone clicked at the other end. Marcel rose from the bed and went to get his coat.

When he stepped out in front of the building fifteen minutes later he saw Marlin down the block. Without waving, or acknowledging that they recognized each other, the two men came towards each other and walked down the sidewalk together.

"I've got my car around the corner. Where do we drive first?"

"I've got an account over at First National near Madison and Thirty-Fourth." They came to the car and got in.

Marcel locked the door on his side, then watched Marlin pull out into the traffic and move to the head of the stream with the skill of a professional. They came to the first bank, and Marcel went in and made out a withdrawal slip for sixty-five hundred in fifties. The cashier looked at the slip, then at him and said, "Are you sure you want this in cash, not a check?"

"Cash, please."

She looked at him curiously, then shrugged and began to count out the amount. Marlin had not come into the bank. He did not take chances on being caught in any circumstance.

When Marcel came out, he held out his hand. "Give it to me here. We go back to the car, then I count it." Marcel handed it over, Marlin pocketed it and they returned to his car. There, the money was counted and Marlin put it into his attache case.

"Okay, what's the next bank?" Marcel named a branch of the Greenwich Bank and they drove there. He was told to take out seven thousand, also in fifties.

After it was counted, Marlin said, "We'd better hurry if we want to hit the last bank on time."

Marcel thought about what it was costing him. Giving away twenty grand for real was a lot harder than saying you would.

At the last bank Marcel took out sixty-five hundred. Here the manager tried to have him keep the account up and even offered him some free gifts to do so. Marcel shook his head, saying he needed the money for some deal he had made and there was no choice.

"At least don't take that much in cash. It could be dangerous." The manager leaned in close.

"Not really. I have a bodyguard with me. I'll be all right."

"If you say so, Mr. Marcel," the bank manager said dubiously, as he walked away from him to his office, looking back a few times. Marcel left the bank and when Marlin asked what had kept him, told what happened.

They returned to the car, the money was counted and when it was done, Marlin shook hands with Marcel. "It's been a pleasure doing business with you, pal. Call again. I'll take you home. You're free now."

Marcel hesitated, and Marlin let go of the ignition key. "What is it, pal? Any questions or doubts?"

"Is there any chance at all they might find out who did it, and then find me through you?"

Marlin sneered. "You're worried I might be traced and then you're worried I might talk. No chance, pal. I've never been caught for a murder. Once for something else. I did time in the pen, but just once. Never since.

"I'm careful. I don't leave fingerprints anyplace. Leave it to me. I won't get caught. By the time they really get into this case I won't be around the city.

"So, relax. You don't have a worry in that direction. I'm all right where it counts. Have a little faith in the guy you just paid twenty thousand dollars."

Marcel looked insecure, but Marlin laughed. "Don't worry. He started the car and pulled out into traffic.

Marcel thought it was the last time he would ever see Mike Marlin or his twenty thousand. While he was not sorry to see the one go, he was about the other.

Chapter Ten

Ryker looked through the new evidence that had come in. There wasn't much. One curious bit was a piece of clear plastic large enough to fit over a pinky that had been found on the chimney platform. He read the report of the lab analysis of the inside of the plastic. Human tissue was recovered and checked, and it was not that of Betty Marcel.

Fischetti stood next to Ryker's desk and asked, "What do you think of that?"

Ryker looked up, thought furrowing his brow. "It's been puzzling you too, huh?" He looked back at the plastic, then said, "It may have been ripped off in the struggle to force Betty Marcel down the chimney. If that's the case, this person wore plastic gloves to hide his fingerprints. This was a planned murder then, not a crime of passion."

"You think it was a hit?" Sal Fischetti asked.

"I can't say. It could have been a disgruntled lover who did this in a fit of rage. The people she knew say she had no lover, but sometimes people lead strange double lives others don't find out about."

Fischetti nodded understandingly, walked away and left Ryker to himself, so he could fill out reports on the day's questioning and events.

Ryker finished his reports quickly, rose from his desk and went to Fischetti's office. Fischetti looked up at he entered.

"You know, Sal, I been thinkin'. Do you suppose Marcel did this?"

"Killed his own wife?"

"Yeah, out of jealousy, because he knew she was fooling around on the side."

"That's a possibility. Why don't you talk to him again?"

"Not today, Sal. I have other things to do. Let him rest. It's been a tough day for him. Nobody should be badgered on the day he finds out his wife is dead, assuming he didn't know beforehand. I know I'm a homicide detective, but I've got a heart."

"You've got a good attitude. All right by me if you wait. Go see what Lindly's doing. I ain't heard from him in an hour."

"I think he went out to get some coffees for himself and the boys."

"Again?" Fischetti exclaimed in annoyance.

"Yeah, that's Lindly for you. He'll be back soon, so don't blow a gasket, Sal. Meanwhile, I'll go looking into the

Carney killing. I still have some unfinished business from last week."

Marlin returned to his room, put down the attache case, got out of his clothes and down to his underwear and stood there in the middle of the room, looking at the twenty thousand dollars. It was all his, like so many other bundles, and it had come so easy.

He'd made some stupid mistakes in his life, but none had tripped him up. Marlin had been a careful man most of the time and that had been his key to success.

He picked up the phone and called down to the desk. He wanted them to send two large cans of beer up to his room. A thin voiced clerk with an accent that was pure New York replied, "We don't serve any beverages here, you know that. You'll have to go out and buy it."

"Can't you send someone to get it? I'll pay for the beers, and five bucks on top of that."

"Five bucks, you say," the voice repeated. "Fine and dandy. I'll have someone get it." Marlin thanked him and hung up.

Marlin put away his money. He would look at it later. At this stage in life the big bundle did not have so much of a thrill for him. You can only be thrilled by a thing so many times.

While waiting for the beer, he paced the room and smoked a cigarette and thought about the new man he would meet, the next job.

He wondered what he would do if he had a wife so terrible that he wanted to get rid of her without the cost and time that divorce takes.

Marlin decided he wouldn't kill her. He would get the divorce and damn the time and money. It surprised him that he thought this way, but it proved he did not know himself as well as he thought he did. Even though the men who hired him were free, they had a burden that would follow them for the rest of their lives.

Marlin saw himself as the angel of death, fulfilling the wishes of some, ending the hopes of others. But he was an angel whose work was for pay, and that made it somewhat sinister.

The knock on the door signaled that his beer was here. He opened the door, went to his pants, got the money to pay for the beers, the five for the man at the desk and an extra fifty cents for the bellhop.

"Here's something you don't have to tell that bastard down there about, fella." The bellhop smiled, touched his cap and was gone.

Marlin closed the door and sat down on his bed. He drank slowly, thinking about his next job. In between kills Marlin had to clear his mind of the last one and think about the new one ahead.

He was halfway through the first beer when another knock came on the door. "Who is it?"

"It's me, Lilly. Why didn't you wait for me to wake up?" Marlin smiled. The bitch was back for more. He got up and let her in.

She came in with a wiggle, her lilac scent preceding her. She was wearing only a housecoat.

"Why didn't you wait for me to get up?"

"I had to go eat and see a man about a prize horse."

"Did you get the horse?"

"Sure did."

"I knocked and you were gone earlier. I thought you'd run out on me after you got what you wanted." She cast a glance down at herself and he followed her eyes.

"I wouldn't run out on you, Lil. I always come back for seconds." They had a laugh at that, then she sat down beside him and he offered her his second beer and a cigarette. They sat smoking and drinking for a few minutes, then she said, "I think I should get out of this thing," meaning the housecoat. "You look so comfortable in your underwear, and I'll be just as comfortable in mine."

Only when she took off her housecoat, there was no underwear, just skin.

Marlin surveyed the spread and said, "That's the kind of underwear I like best." He put down his beer can and stubbed out his cigarette. They embraced slowly, with smoldering passion, like lovers who had known each other awhile. The first probing kiss was followed by a longer, unending one that served to touch off their lust and the act of mutual seduction was on.

Ryker returned from the report room, a section off the main office complex, where files of new murders were piled on a wooden table. It was marked by long, dark cigarette burns and the scratches of pens and files.

What he saw stopped him. There were two more unsolved murders in the file list, one a fifty-two year old housewife and the other a forty-nine year old housewife.

Ryker thought about it awhile, shrugged and went back to his desk. Lindly returned with coffee. "You're taking it easy," Ryker told him.

"There's really nothing much to do yet, unless you want to go back and talk to Marcel again."

"Not today. I want to let him rest. I told Sal and he agreed. Tomorrow we talk to him."

Marcel dialed Sylvie's number, listened to the ring before she picked up the phone at the other end. "Hello, who is this?"

"This is Eddie."

"Oh, sweetheart, good to hear from you. I missed you. You should have called earlier. Where are you calling from?"

"Home. I just wanted to hear your voice."

"Betty isn't home, Eddie. Otherwise you wouldn't dare call except from the office. Why haven't you been to the office these last few days? I decided to take off today."

"That's why I called. I knew you'd be home. It was agony not calling you."

"With Betty around, that's the way it has to be sugar."

"Not now. Betty won't be bothering us any more."

"What do you mean? Has she left you?" Sylvie exclaimed.

"No, she was murdered. The police don't know by whom yet, but they'll find out. I spoke with two detectives and they look like they know what they're doing."

"How did she die, Eddie?"

"In a very horrible manner. I don't want to discuss it with you. I don't want to hurt you, Sylvie, I just want to enjoy your company and I want you to enjoy mine. This means I'm free, Sylvie, free to marry you. Not right away, of course. I mean, I have to put up a front of mourning, but after it's over we can marry."

She listened to the mad, passionate rush of words and answered, "This is so quick. I hadn't thought this would ever happen. Oh, Eddie, I don't know what to say. It surprises me that you should not be upset that your wife is dead. Would you think that way about me, too?" she asked. Dames, he thought.

"Of course not, Sylvie. I didn't love her, so her death hasn't affected me that much. But you—I care about you."

"I understand. When can I see you, Eddie?"

"Not now. Her relatives will be over. There will be mourning. The police will be over. Not yet. I'll call and tell you when. Till then, I'll be in touch. I'll be in the office to see how business is doing, and you can come over from your office, it's only across the hall. You can visit your friend Ruth, and sort of stop by to say hello when things slack off."

"I know the routine by now, Eddie. Bye, baby. Don't let Betty's death get you down." He laughed out loud in the phone. As he was laughing, she hung up.

Sylvie Weinstock turned to the dark-haired man beside her on the living room couch. She nodded toward the phone. "That was my fat boy friend, Eddie. You know, when you're out of town, he keeps me busy, takes me out to swell places. A funny fat guy, but nice to be with when no one else is around and it's lonely."

"You don't have to tell me how it is," her boy friend said, as he leaned over and they embraced.

Marcel was dialing Betty's mother. It was time to break the sad news and have all the crying relatives over. It was an ordeal he would steel himself for, but he could do it. For Sylvie he could do a lot more. It had already cost him twenty thousand dollars and the life of his wife. The more he thought about it, the more he realized it was worth it.

Chapter Eleven

Marlin had finished with his go-go girl, who had dressed and gone off to wiggle her butt at customers so they would stay and buy more glasses of watered-down beer.

Marlin had also dressed, and went down to the lobby, nodded at the desk man and stepped out into the cool gray darkness of Manhattan by night.

His car was parked on one of the dark side streets. Two small kids were fooling around with the door. Marlin didn't make a move till he was behind them, so they would think he was just one of the passers-by. When he was close enough he put his foot on both their asses, so fast it was a blur. They were hopping up and down as they ran down the sidewalk, rubbing their behinds.

Satisfied, Marlin unlocked the car and started the motor. He pulled out into the traffic and drove over to the west Forties, found the Ryder Theater and parked nearby.

He looked for Matilda's Restaurant, where he would meet Wilbur Purcell. It was a fairly clean establishment, as places in this area went.

There was a flashing pink neon sign you couldn't miss from blocks away and a series of tables for two and four in long rows all the way to the back, plastic potted palms and mirror walls. In the back was a man in a brown suit with a dark blue wool overcoat hung over the chair on his right. He was drinking what looked to be a coffee in a brown mug, but Marlin knew it was hot chocolate. Poagie Reeves had told him so and Poagie did not lie.

Marlin looked at his watch. The pale pink neon illuminated his face and made him look sickly. He went to the restaurant door and stepped inside.

A thick steamy warmth hit him. Marlin had to take off his hat and wipe his forehead. The other man was looking down into his steaming chocolate, waiting for it to cool. Marlin remembered his line and approached Purcell's table.

As Marlin walked towards him, Purcell looked up. He was a tall man in his early sixties, with a lined, weathered face. They had made eye contact long before Marlin reached the table, and though they spoke the agreed upon words, they did not need to.

"Is the hot chocolate here good?" Marlin asked, nodding towards the brownish goo in the mug.

"Reasonably so, try some," Purcell answered in a gravelly voice. Marlin sat down across from him.

"My name is Purcell," The white-haired man told him,

visibly nervous, his palms sweaty.

"I know your name. Call me Mike. We both know Poagy and no other introduction has to be made. Why don't we get down to business."

"Yes, why don't we?" Purcell echoed. He bit his lip in hesitation and looked at Marlin a few times, then down into his coffee. Marlin hated these meetings—so slow to start, the client so reluctant to get to the subject, but he dared not push hard. There was money in this and for twenty thousand dollars a man can take a lot.

Purcell did not hesitate as long as some others. He looked up and said, "I hate my wife. She's a shrew and makes each day a nightmare, and each night a super-nightmare. She's got me so that I'm taking tranquilizers and drink, sometimes both. It interferes with my work, costs me money and at times affects my business. I can't take it. I want out. I don't want her replaced by another woman, I just want her gone.

"I'll pay whatever it takes. In this case twenty thousand dollars, isn't it?" He looked up, afraid it would cost more, but showing by the tone of his voice and his actions that he would pay whatever it took.

Marlin was tempted for a moment to say it was twenty-five, but knew he could not get this price all the time, and having once got it, working for less would bother him. He nodded that it was twenty thousand.

"When do you want it?"

"After I hit. I never ask for money beforehand. There's always a chance the job might be bungled, and then I'd have the money and the client would have no satisfaction. Not that I've ever botched a kill. All I require from you is a description of the victim, name, age, habits, where she likes to go and how she likes to spend her time. This way I can follow her and see when and where it would be best to kill her. When that's done, you pay me." A noisy couple started to sit down two tables from them. The scraping of chairs drew their attention for a moment, and then they turned back to the topic.

"Let's discuss money first," Purcell suggested.

"Fine with me, Mr. Purcell. If that's what you want to discuss, then that's what I want to discuss too. As you've heard, I take twenty. I always like it in cash. The bills should be small denominations. I don't take hundreds, they're too conspicuous. So I insist on fifties."

Purcell agreed. "That part I can take care of. I'd give you a check," Purcell smiled, "but I understand how it is. I see no difficulty in that part. Where the difficulty comes is in getting rid of my wife. You can do it?"

Marlin nodded up and down. "In almost twenty-five years I have yet to meet a dissatisfied customer, and you won't be the first. Now how old is your wife?"

Purcell put a hand in the air. "About my age."

"Does she look it?" Marlin wanted to know.

"Yes, she looks it pretty much. In fact, if I may say so, she looks older than me." He settled back in his chair, a look of malicious joy filling his face.

"How does your wife look? Where does she usually like to go?"

In answer Purcell put down his mug, removed a pigskin wallet from his pocket and took out a small black-and-white snapshot, which he tossed on the formica tabletop.

Marlin saw a woman around Purcell's age. She had pepper and salt hair swept up from the back and piled atop her head. Her mouth was downcast and shrewish, her nose long and probing. Marlin did not have to wonder why Purcell would want her six feet under and himself free of her clutches.

He handed the picture back. "Like what you see?" the

man asked.

"Mr. Purcell, I don't like or dislike anything. I just do what I'm paid to do."

"If that's the way you look at it, I can't argue with you. I'm just the man that pays the bill. And when I pay, I like to know I'm dealing with someone competent."

"Competence is what you'll get. As I've said, I have almost twenty-five years in this business. I can't fail and you can't fail. Now what are her habits?"

"She likes to nag, nag, nag and make my life miserable. After that she likes to spend my money like water. If I complain she dishes out criticism, sarcasm and slurs. Adelaide says things you wouldn't believe. My wife generally leaves the house an hour or two after I leave for work at nine. She will spend the morning shopping at Bonwit Teller, Saks Fifth Avenue, Bloomingdale's, maybe a few shoe shops. She might stop in at Mr. Cyril's Beauty Salon, just down the street from Saks. I don't know why. Nothing could help her regain her beauty.

"Now, as I said, she shops around and then about one-thirty, two, may stop off for a late lunch at Sardi's. Know where that is?" Marlin nodded.

"After Sardi's she may stop off at a book store on Fifth Avenue. She may come home three or four in the afternoon, with a few paperback mysteries to read. My wife loves mysteries, devours them."

"I think I have enough now, Mr. Purcell. I'll be taking my leave. You should hear from me within a week. I like to follow my victim around a while, see the lay of things, plot my moves, then stirke. When I call, you'll meet me alone, needless to say, and we'll go get the money."

Purcell nodded. They shook hands. You don't sign contracts with hit men.

Chapter Twelve

Ryker looked at the TV and sniggered. The private eye was going through a lot of false heroics in order to rescue a maiden in distress. It was a stale plot in a stale series that would not be successful despite the hamming of the star and the exertions of the writers and director.

Ryker shut the TV in the middle of a fist fight. They were so common they put him to sleep.

Now he had a whole evening ahead of him and nothing to do. He thought about the case he was on, the horrible murder, that the newspapers now knew about. He looked at the fresh copy of the *News* on his coffee table. It was open to page three, was a short blurb about the killing and the fact that the police knew nothing. The reporter ended it with the usual spiel about citizens being alarmed.

Ryker lit one of the thin, black cigars he liked to smoke. He mulled over the case and a thought struck him as if someone whispered in his ear. This was a professional kill, not a murder done by someone that loved and then hated her. Someone who had been involved with a woman would do her in on a date, in a place like a lovers' lane, in rage, not with cool professionalism.

The more Ryker thought about it, the less it seemed likely that an enraged boy friend could coldly meet her after work, point a gun at her, march her into the lobby of another building, into the elevator, up to the top floor and hold her there while he cut the chain that barred entrance to the roof. After which he would take her up, at gunpoint presumably and make her climb the platforms to the chimney base, put his gun away and cold-bloodedly shove her down.

It could be believed if one assumed a boy friend could keep up his cool for that long period without the fear of someone coming, her running or screaming, or his nerve breaking. Nobody, no matter how angry, could keep his nerve while doing all that. It took a cool customer to negotiate the barriers and commit the murder. A boy friend or husband did not fit the bill. It seemed to be a premeditated act.

He met her on the street. Perhaps they argued. He pulled the gun. The street was deserted. The area is a business district, not a place where people would congregate at that time of night.

Once he got her up onto the roof, if he had a gun he could have shot her and left her there. That would be the most logical thing, Ryker thought.

He would be hysterical, anxious to get it over with. That would be the best way. Another would be to push her off the roof. The third way would be to push her into the chimney.

Ryker's mind was alive with theories. He picked up the phone and called Fischetti, still at the office. Ryker gave him a quick rundown of what he'd been thinking.

"You don't say, Joe. You may have something there. Can you get your ass over here? I've got nothing to do. I'm willing to stay overtime. What about you? We can think this through, throw around some ideas. I like your line, Joe. It's wonderful what you can do when you take your brain out of storage."

"Oh, shut up, Sal. I'll be over in a little while." Ryker hung up and reached for his trench coat.

They got coffee, lit up smokes and were soon throwing around ideas as if they had nothing else in the world to do.

"So it's your contention he held a gun on her, this mystery man, and took her up to the roof and then you listed the three options he had of killing her. What makes you think he had a gun?"

"If he'd had a knife, the only way he could take her up to the roof would be to hold it to her throat and they would look pretty obvious going through the lobby and up in the elevator like that.

"If you have a gun you can always hold it in your pocket, poke it in her back and keep her from running away in case someone enters the elevator. A knife you have to keep in the open, if you poke it in someone's back they can still get away from you by running forward. Let's say the elevator door opens and someone comes in, you run out, away from the man with the knife. He may run after you and take the risk of someone calling the police or jumping on him, but you can try and get away and possibly make it.

"The pressure would be great on anyone bringing her up to the roof if he's got a gun, but even worse with a knife. Take my word, it was a gun."

"Okay," Fischetti said. "It was a gun. Now from there, how do you decide this guy isn't an enraged husband or lover, but someone else, a really tough character?"

"A prepared character," Ryker replied. "That thick wire door to the roof was chained shut. He used a chain cutter. None was around, our men checked with the superintendent. This character had one with him. That meant he was prepared for an obstacle, or knew he was going to take the woman to this particular roof.

"If he was that prepared, he was cool. He knew a knife wouldn't do as much good as a gun. If he was prepared, he knew that going up in the elevator meant taking a chance on being seen. If he was smart, he walked her up those fire stairs. We've got to check the stairs from top to bottom to see if anything that belonged to Betty Marcel or the killer was dropped on those stairs."

"We'll check, Joe. I can get the car now. We'll be there in—wait, it's locked for the night. But there's a watchman, he'll let us in."

"If he's not sleeping off a pint of cheap wine. This can wait till tomorrow, Sal. There's probably nothing there anyway. For now let's take our reasoning to its logical conclusion. If there is a strain on a man, any man, who takes this woman to the roof to kill her as planned, wouldn't he want to be rid of the strain right away?"

"Of course," Fischetti answered, stroking the side of his head. "As soon as possible. That's the way I'd do it."

"He'd shoot her, then. That's quick. Who'd hear up on

116

that roof, with the wide outdoors to swallow the sound? He'd shoot her and go."

"But this character doesn't. After all the strain of getting her up there, all the cajoling and threats, he doesn't shoot her, he doesn't shove her off the edge of the roof, but he makes her climb several platforms to the chimney base, which is hard on her and him. Remember, he has to urge her forward and has to climb up after her, making sure he can always reach his gun and be extra alert so she doesn't kick him in the face.

"Then he puts his gun away and shoves her down the chimney, which is even more of a struggle than shoving her off the roof. That takes cool, tough cool.

"It can't be a psychopath. This requires cleverness and cool emotion. A psychopath's basic mental failings would catch up with him under that strain.

"No, Sal. What we are dealing with is a hired killer, a good one. This woman was hit."

The men looked at each other across the desk. Fischetti stubbed out his cigarette and shook his head.

"The hypothesis sounds good. I can't argue, Joe. But we need proof. Even if I'm willing to accept this, as far as it goes, you have to link this to someone. Hired killers don't grow on trees. They cost money. Somebody has to hire them."

"Exactly," Ryker answered. "That's what we'll tackle next. Somewhere there's a pattern, and I think we're beginning to find threads of it tonight. This killer was not someone off the street. The way he operated shows he knew what he was doing. He was too good and experienced to be just anyone. No, this is a pro killer, a boy with a lot of experience. That means he cost money."

"So," Fischetti concluded, "it couldn't have been a boy friend. He would be mad enough to kill, but maybe not mad enough to pay a pro to do it for him. I'd tag the husband. He has money, a lot, according to the report on his income taxes."

The two men absorbed that. "I think we had better go see Mr. Marcel," Fischetti said.

"Wait, I'd like to check his bank accounts to see if he took out any large amounts recently, and any stocks or bonds, to see if he cashed anything to make the kind of money he'd need for a hired gun."

"I can do that for you, Joe. I'll have to put through the request. We can have it by tomorrow afternoon. If it is Marcel, I'd like to know who the gun is."

"I have a theory about that, too, Sal."

"Let's hear it."

"Those two other women who were murdered, and who are in about the same age range as Betty Marcel, and whose murders have not yet been solved could have been killed by the same man."

"I think you mentioned this to Lindly and we discussed this earlier today. You felt then that all three killings were linked by some maniac."

"Not now. At least not the kind of maniac you might be thinking of. This man is a maniac, but in a rather distant sense."

"Well, he's the kind of man whose conscience and morals have been warped so far that he no longer feels any remorse about what he does. It's a job, like killing chickens to a slaughterer. You know."

"Yes, I see, but that's speculation. Show me some facts to support this. That's what we need."

"Their age range. I know that isn't much, but it's a starting point. We can check what the husbands of these women do for a living. My contention is they are all well-to-do men who had a lot to lose by divorcing their wives, but wanted them out of the way. See?"

"I do," Fischetti told him. "You know, this whole thing could be linked. If it is, there's a pro out there somewhere—tough, smart and dangerous. And that makes our job even harder. Pros don't leave any tracks."

"Yes, they do," Ryker answered. "They leave a lot of tracks. These men have to get to know the husbands of the women they are to kill, they have to arrange a contract and they have to be paid. All we have to do is find the pay terminals, the places where contacts are made. Then we'll have our killer."

Fischetti guffawed. "There are eight million slobs out there, and you have to find out which one did it. You can't stop everyone on the street."

"I know," Ryker said. "And if I could ask most of the people, I wouldn't. They're too dumb to know what's going on around them. We have to know where to go and that takes deductive logic."

Fischetti pointed to him. "You're the man with the deductive logic. Where are you going to lead us?"

"First, I want an idea of the financial condition of the husbands of the two women who died before Betty Marcel. Run a check to see if there have been any other murders in that area in the last three months."

"What are the names of the two women?" Fischetti asked as he bent over a pad with pen in hand.

Ryker slapped at his head. "Let me think. Mildred Essex and Connie Wilcox. One was killed two and a half weeks back and the other about five or six weeks ago. One jumped or was pushed off a roof in Forest Hills and the other died when her car went out of control on Northern Boulevard and crashed into a lightpost. It toppled the pole and went on up over the sidewalk, through a chain fence and into a small lawn piled with garbage cans."

"You remember the details pretty well," Fischetti said.

"I didn't think I would, but now that all this has been laid out, I suggest we start looking. If my hunch is right, Edward Marcel and the husbands of the other two woman may have paid one hit man to do the job. My suspicion is that it involves a group of individuals who connected these men with the killer."

Fischetti rose from his chair and said, "Let's go to the records room and see if there's any information on the husbands of those women. If this hunch proves right, Ryker, you've got yourself a citation, if not a raise."

"I'll take the raise," Ryker said, as they left Fischetti's office. "I can buy groceries with a raise."

Chapter Thirteen

Marlin didn't go straight home. He walked the streets of the city. The gritty sidewalk, smoke coming from manhole covers, smog from the cars and trucks and taxis and gaily colored neon flashing in his face. He stopped in for franks and a coke at a small stand, then moved on.

Tonight, he did not feel like walking far, and returned to the hotel. Lilly was gone, wiggling her ass in the Purple Panther. He could go see her, but didn't want to. Besides sex, she had little to offer him.

He switched on the TV and tried watching an old

gangster movie. It left him cold. He shut the TV and looked around at the room. It cost him thirty-five dollars a week. Soon he would dump it and go to another place and rent another room there at about the same price. After a few months he would go to another city and rent a room there.

When he figured it out, Marlin put twenty-five hundred dollars every year into rent. He hadn't really thought much about it in the past, spending without really thinking. Now he was getting to an age where he thought about that and a lot of other things. He figured that eating out was costing him an average of seven dollars a day, even when he didn't splurge and eat good suppers and take women out. That too came out to about twenty-five hundred a year, if not more. In rent and food he was spending about one quarter of his fee for one hit.

What bothered him was moving around from place to place, the tension at one time, complete boredom at another. Three times each year now, he'd move to another city. It was not safe to spend a long time in one town. He would not return to the same town for two or three years if he could help it.

One third of each year he spent resting. He was getting tired of Florida, so he might go to Maine and spend his summers there. It was certainly worth looking into.

One day, when he grew too old and could no longer perform, he would retire and buy himself a fine home. A place that was real and his, not like a hotel room.

He got his jacket and decided to go downtown again. He could hit a movie, then a Chinese place for some chow mein and egg rolls, then a stroll through the porno shops, after which he'd be ready for Lilly again. Seeing her then would be a pleasure.

Ryker and Fischetti sifted through the data that lay on

the desk between them. The husbands of all three murdered women were wealthy, all in the seventy thousand bracket.

So this too linked up well. Men who were tired of their wives after twenty years of marriage had discovered a way of killing the marriage but saving money. Divorce was out—too expensive. Murder is faster, less scandalous, cheaper by far. So it had been murder that had decided the time and place for the marriage to be terminated.

Talking to the husbands would get them nowhere. They would deny everything. The only one they might talk to would be Edward Marcel. He was still in the middle of the muddle, not yet emotionally stable enough to evade tough questions.

"We can take him down here and question him," Ryker said.

"He'll get a good lawyer," Fischetti answered. "You have no idea what a great effort he'll make."

"Let him. He can't save a bad situation from falling apart in his face."

"Yeah, tomorrow morning we'll bring him down here. Meanwhile, where the hell did these three people get their hit man?"

"From some hoodlum. But where would they know hoodlums from? The method of operation here was professional and similar enough to have been done by one man. He would have to have been hired through an underworld contact. I can see one of these husbands knowing a gangster through some childhood acquaintance, but not all three. It would have to be a light contact, someone they could talk to and who would connect them to somebody else."

Fischetti snapped his fingers. "A bookie, that's who. They used bookies, they knew them well. You'd be surprised how many of these rich bastards gamble. They

123

throw their money away on the ponies, football, ask around for other things—a dame, a hot card party, a hit man. The bookie knows them well and wants to keep them, so he asks around, gets told where the action is and tells them a number to call."

"Wouldn't the mob take it on?" Ryker asked.

"No," Fischetti shook his head. "They're afraid the guy might talk if the police check. Then they'd be in trouble. They would let it go to an independent. Somebody who's here today, gone tomorrow."

"Who would the independents be?"

"Good ones? There're only a few. They spend a few months in a city, piling up several kills and then they disappear," Fischetti answered.

"But they should get caught, the police should notice a pattern."

"Not necessarily, Joe. The police don't link every crime. We're too busy. There are variations in the way the killings are done. There are times the body is not found. The body we did find could just as well have burned up without being noticed. A man like that seldom leaves tracks. For instance, let's say he kills only eight people in a city and three bodies are never found. We might connect only one or two of the murders, and by the time we connect the rest, he's gone. Many of these people have never been seen. We know them only by the way they operate.

"By the time a dozen people are dead we know his method, but even then, it's not easy to find people. The husbands won't talk, the guys who connect the husbands and the killers won't talk. So we face a stone wall of silence. It's seldom you hear of someone like this being caught, Joe. I don't think I've ever seen one caught in my time on the force and I don't have much hope that I will."

"Don't say that, Sal. You have me." Ryker was barely

able to duck the paperweight Fischetti threw in his direction as he jumped from his seat.

Marcel offered Betty's mother a piece of sponge cake. Her father sat on the couch, his wrinkled face expressing a sorrow no words could express. Several neighbors, some people from his firm, a few relatives from her side were in the room. The bedroom door had been closed, her picture, taken in happier times, was on the coffee table and her mother would go to it, look down sadly, smile a weak smile, then pick it up and clutch it to her bosom. A tear would escape her closed eyes, run down her wrinkled cheek and drop off onto her sagging bosom.

Marcel looked away. It hurt him too much. Her father just sat there like a lump most of the time, and when he did speak, moaned that it was a sad day for him that he had outlived his child, that he had lived to see his child murdered in such a manner.

He would talk of his little Betty and how she had been such a bright and pretty little girl. Marcel would look away and say to himself, if she was so sweet, how come she grew up to be such a bitch. Their love had been strong when he was young and had nothing, only the shirt on his back and a willingness to go out and make a life for the two of them.

She had loved him then, and she had been behind him all the way. Later she grew cold towards him, when the good times were on them she refused to help him, refused to be the wife she had been when they were young. So his heart turned from her and he looked for another, and found Sylvie.

Sylvie. His lips almost smiled when he thought of her. His mind cautioned him not to smile and he bit his lips and turned back to the others. Soon, this crap would be over and he could call Sylvie and be with her, feel the sweetness of her thighs. But for now, he must play the part and wait.

The coroner would soon release her body and they would bury it. The funeral would cost him another pretty penny, but that would be the last money he would ever spend on Betty.

"Eddie." It was Betty's sister Sarah, older than her, taller, uglier. He had always hated her.

"Yeah, what do you want Sarah?"

"Get the other bottle of Canadian scotch, you know the one you put away." She knew everything, this bitch. Betty didn't leave out one detail.

"Get the bottle, Eddie. There are going to be more people coming to offer their condolences and we'll run short." She lifted the bottle and swished around the small amount of whiskey left.

Oh, to be with Sylvie. To be sticking it into her. To be enjoying her now. He went to the kitchen cabinet where he kept the liquor and opened it. He took out the bottle, noticed two others were gone and realized the people had been guzzling it faster than he thought.

He brought the bottle into the foyer and immediately Sarah began to slit the top open. He turned from her and went to sit on the couch next to her father.

They looked at each other. "Eddie, what have you got to say?"

"What can I say, pa. What can I say when I lose the best and sweetest woman I've known. There's a lot I can say." He touched his chest. "But my heart is too full."

The effect was good. The old man blinked twice and shook his ponderous head up and down and then looked back down at his big belly, sagging down on the couch.

Eddie looked at his belly also. You're too fat, pa. You should go on a diet. But telling you that is like telling your daughter not to do something. She wouldn't listen. She was like you, pa, stubborn. You two were cut from one piece. Made for each other. She was like you and you are like she was. Betty wasn't a sweet woman. Had she been a good wife, she'd be here today still. But she's where she belongs, where all bad wives belong.

Her mother was crying again. Marcel felt a twinge of pity, but not for long. Her mother, to him, was a hated figure.

He looked at Betty's sister filling the cut glass whiskey glasses and cutting cubes of sponge cake for the people still to come. An urge almost overcame him. He wanted to rise up and run from here, call Sylvie and sit with her on a bench in Central Park, visit the zoo and feed the pigeons and to talk about the things people in love talk about.

Instead, he held himself in check. He listened to the low voices, and looked at the long faces. Her father let out a gust of air, shook his head up and down, then became silent again.

Her mother sobbed softly, to herself almost, wiping her eyes with the edge of a napkin. Sarah came over to Marcel. She looked down at him, the displeasure in her face almost as pronounced as the tone of her voice. Her pose clearly asked, Why her and not you? He waited for her to speak.

"You have any other bottles in the house?"

He pointed at a portable bar in the living room. "In there. We have some half and quarter full bottles of whiskey. All sorts."

"Haven't you got any full bottles?" He put his palms up and shrugged. "More people will be coming and there just won't be enough. There's enough cake, but not enough whiskey."

"Forget it, Sarah. This isn't Duffy's Tavern. Serve 'em soda."

"Eddie, I'm ashamed of you," she said in a loud voice.

Heads turned. "Your beloved wife is dead and you speak this way." She wasn't so beloved, my dear. If you knew what I paid to get rid of her, you'd know.

All he said was, "It's your sister's funeral. Shouldn't you be worrying about other things than whiskey bottles?" Sarah went off in a huff. She disappeared before her mother could put a hand out to stop the argument. Her father just sat and stared and said nothing.

The low talking in the room began to pick up again. Then two neighbors of theirs, the Browns, from the floor below stepped up to him. They were nice people, he had met them only a few times and yet they had stopped in to offer condolences.

Mr. Brown was a tall, balding man, with a pot belly and a soft smile. Marcel rose. They shook hands and Brown once again offered his sympathy and said how he hoped the police would find the killer soon.

"I'm hoping that too," Marcel answered. "Day and night I wait for their call, just praying they'll find the killer."

"I certainly hope so," Mr. Brown said. He was seconded by his wife. Marcel walked them to the door, held it open and bid them goodbye as they left. He closed the door, blew out air between his clenched teeth to dissipate the tension and went on back to the others.

He almost bumped into Sarah, coming back from the living room with the half-full whiskey bottles in her arms.

Chapter Fourteen

Ryker, Fischetti and Lindly were waiting for reports from the banks on the financial conditions of the husbands of the three dead women.

It was ten-thirty when the reports came in. They gathered in Fischetti's office and sat around the desk, passing the papers back and forth. They were concise and to the point, and boded ill for the three husbands involved, or rather the three widowers.

All had assets well above one hundred thousand dollars, and all had recently removed twenty thousand dollars from various banks.

"Let me have the dates of each killing," Ryker asked Lindly. He compared the date of each murder to the date on which the withdrawals were made.

"What do you have?" Lindly wanted to know.

"Each murder date is followed by a withdrawal of money. If the killing was on the fifth, the withdrawal was on the sixth. It's too great a similarity to be a coincidence."

"That means they were all killed by the same hit man," Lindly concluded. "Some guys would want the money beforehand, or half before and half after. This guy was so good he didn't ask for a cent till after the job. He was that sure of success."

"Exactly," Ryker answered. "I'd like to go see the husband of the first woman that was killed. Have him brought in."

Fischetti raised the phone to his ear and made two calls. When he put the phone back in the cradle he said, "He'll be here in an hour. He has a firm over in Long Island City. They'll pick him up and bring him here. No reason we should travel."

An hour later, almost to the minute, they brought in Robert Essex, widower of Mildred Essex. He was a woman chaser by looks, the owner of his own industrial advertising firm.

He smelled of whiskey when they brought him into the conference room, put him at the head of the table like some honored guest and sat down on either side. He was already uncomfortable and drummed the formica tabletop with his fingers. This room was quite often used for interrogation and Ryker felt at home in it.

They began to ask questions. He answered slowly, calmly, mostly in monosyllables. They had told him his rights and asked if he wanted a lawyer, but he declined.

"What have I got to hide?" he asked. Then they showed him the financial report that told of the twenty thousand dollar withdrawal. He lost some of his self confidence.

"Well?" Fischetti wanted to know.

"Nothing. I took out twenty thousand."

"What for?" Ryker asked. "You'd better not say it was to buy stock. We'll check. You can't tell us it was for a car, because we'll want to see the car and know what dealer you bought it from."

"If you said it was a dame," Ryker added, "and you were going to hire her services for a week, I could understand. You're a strong, vigorous guy with needs and your wife is gone. But not twenty thousand. Now tell me. I'm interested, and this had better be good."

"I go to the bookies. I can't tell you which. If I did I'd be in trouble, because you would check and they'd be in trouble. Then I'd be salami and they'd be the slicer. All I'll say is that I owed them money. I piled up debts, they pressed me to pay and I did."

"All on one day?"

"That's right, Sergeant Ryker. All on one day. Things like this happen."

Ryker threw a list on the desk. "Go on, read it." Essex picked it up and read through it. His brutal face began to change, then fell back into a nonchalant pose.

"That, Mr. Essex, is a list of two other men, rich like yourself. Their wives died too. We haven't found the killer. They also had gambling debts, twenty thousand exactly. Their wives died one day, the next day they took twenty thousand out of the bank. So did you. That, Mr. Essex, is a pattern so suspicious the Deputy Inspector would have my badge if I let you out of here. I'm arresting you on suspicion of planning to murder your wife and paying a professional to do it. Book him, Lindly."

Essex rose out of his seat like a volcano. "Wait one goddamn minute, mister. I'm innocent. You can't do this. I'm a respectable businessman."

"They all say that. As for what I can and can't do, ask your lawyer when he comes to see you. He'll tell you that the first thing you never do is speak to a cop without a lawyer. You had the chance to have him here and you blew it. And now you'll suffer for it."

As he was saying this a patrolman came into the room. Ryker turned to him. "Take this gentleman to the detention cell. Have him give you the name of his lawyer. Call him and tell him to get over here. Or would you prefer to call him?" Ryker asked as he turned back to Essex.

For a second Essex didn't answer, then he said, "I'll call. Show me where the phone is." He turned and walked out of the room ahead of the policeman.

"What happens now?" Lindly wanted to know.

"His lawyer will get him out. We'll pull Essex in front of the judge and ask for bail. Make it a hundred thousand."

"You'll never get it," Fischetti said. "This guy is an honest businessman, or supposedly honest. Honest men don't have their wives murdered by hit men. Anyway, the judge will treat him that way. The most we can get is twenty-five thousand."

"Not bad," Ryker said. "He'll go to a bail bondsman and get it. Then he'll owe the bondsman twelve-fifty. They ask for five percent of the bail as payment. Twelve hundred odd bucks is a loss he'll feel."

"Not if he's paid out twenty thousand already," Lindly said. "And you know, Joe, he just might have lost that money in a gambling spree."

Ryker shook his head. "This pattern is too good. I can feel it in my bones. This guy is our man. So are the other two. But I want to play with this one awhile."

"Why, Joe?" Fischetti asked.

"We've accused this guy of serious things. Being human he wants to show us we're wrong even if we're right. How does he do this? He goes to the bookie who put him in touch with the killer. He says to the bookie that he has trouble. The police suspect him. He tells the bookie how he explained away the twenty thousand. He needs corroborating testimony. If the bookie will say he took the twenty thousand for gambling debts, Essex will be free of suspicion.

"The bookie won't want to. Essex will plead that he'll get the police to make a deal to take his testimony without using the fact that he's a bookie against him. What could one favor hurt him? Would another twenty thousand be enough for a favor?"

"You mean he'd pay?" Bo Lindly asked.

"Sure. Wouldn't you, if your ass was in a sling?"

"But he'll have to withdraw another twenty thousand. We'd know."

"Not necessarily. He'd promise to pay later, after we're gone. Or else he would borrow from some businessmen friends. He'd sign notes and owe them the payment in services, for which they'd just deduct the money they owed him instead of paying each time. We'd never know unless we put in a big search, and we wouldn't if he convinced us he was innocent."

"Yeah, but we haven't got anything," Lindly said. "We have to find the killer and that's hard with hit men."

"This time it'll be different. I don't care what Essex's plans are, or how he goes about them. I do know he'll try to see the bookie. The bookie won't go along with his crazy scheme. When he hears about this, he'll want to see Essex. We have him tailed, we find the bookie. End of part one.

"Once we know who the bookie is we have our next

opening. He will call the man who told him about the killer. I know how these people work. He just won't let it lie without saying anything."

"Then if something happens, they'll blame him." The others nodded agreement and Ryker explained how he was going to get all the links leading to the killer.

"When he tells the party that he can't speak over the phone because the matter is quite delicate, the party will understand and get together with him. We tail the bookie. End of part two.

"This party will lead us to the killer. We move in and apprehend, or shoot to kill if he gives a struggle. End of part three. Then, of course, we apprehend the three husbands and get confessions eventually. I don't think it'll be too much trouble then, even with their lawyers running tackle. End of part four, and end of the case for us. The D.A. will take care of the rest, along with most of the glory. We'll be called upon to testify and for us that will be all there is to it."

Fischetti punched the palm of one hand with the other, went around to the head of the table and put his hands down on the rim of the chair Essex had sat in. "Let's hope you're right, Joe. I sure hope it goes that way. If it does I'm happy and you're happy."

"Yeah," Lindly joined in. "We get a raise."

Chapter Fifteen

Marlin followed Mrs. Purcell from store to store, from the beauty parlor to Smith's, a high class food store. He followed her home, then just sat and waited down the street from her house for her to appear again. Sometimes they did, sometimes they didn't.

At four in the afternoon Mrs. Purcell left her apartment house, hailed a cab and drove uptown to a movie theater. She was going to see an Italian detective thriller called "Four Dead Flies on Velvet."

Marlin noted when she went in, picked up his copy of

the *News*, looked for the theater, found the times the picture started and ended. He knew when to come back and drove off to the waterfront. He could read his paper and come back.

Assuming she liked the picture and didn't walk out in the middle, he would catch her coming out and follow her from there. Mrs. Purcell certainly had expensive habits. If Marlin had a wife who looked like that, made his life miserable and threw money around like confetti, he too would get rid of her.

The only thing that surprised Marlin was that the men married to these women waited so long before they gave them the heave-ho. Had they done this when they were younger, they could have married some young cutie and enjoyed life a little. But when they were younger, they didn't have the money or didn't have enough brains to realize they were losing time.

They came to Marlin now, with fists full of money, in the autumn of their careers, asking to be free of the burdens that had now become unbearable.

The time passed almost before he knew it. He threw the paper out of his window and started the car.

Marlin drove by just as she was coming out among the crowd of moviegoers. She headed down the street, turned in at the end of the block. Marlin continued up the block and turned at the corner, went down the side street fast so he could circle the block and come up the street she had just gone down.

He saw her turn, walk down several flights of stairs and pull open he door of a bar. It was one of those fancy, fashionable bars Manhattan is full of.

Marlin circled the block again, looking for parking on the less populated side streets. He found a space, put a dime in the meter and went to the bar.

He sighted her as soon as he stepped into the reddish, dim glow. She wasn't at a table, but by the long mahogany bar with pink lighted glass shelves and bottles.

He sat down a few seats down from her and ordered a whiskey sour. It was three bucks. This was an expensive place, he thought.

He had not been sitting more than a few minutes when she started to talk to him. He was so surprised that for a minute he said nothing, then pointed to himself and said, "Me?" as if he didn't know.

"Is there anyone else around?" She looked behind him and he looked too. She had a New England accent and after the beauty parlor and in this light didn't look so bad, but on the other hand, she wasn't that good. Better than the photo her husband had shown him.

It struck him that she was trying to pick him up. This old broad was hot for young guys. It was ludicrous he hadn't thought of it before.

"What's your name, handsome?" she was being coy like a schoolgirl. She sure didn't waste time either.

"James, James Roy. What's yours?" She got up off her chair and came to sit beside him, a smile on her kisser a yard wide.

"My name is Connie." Liar, he thought. "This is a dump." She motioned with her head to the bar. "Why don't we go someplace else?" Marlin smiled but not for that reason. Here was his pigeon, just asking to be cooked. He had the car. A quick drive, a fast strangle and it was over.

"I've got my car two blocks away."

"Great," she said slowly, then put her arm through his. "Let's depart." A few guys seeing them sniggered. They must think I'm hard up, he thought. The hell with them.

Out in daylight she did not look as good as in the bar. The wrinkles and lines in her face showed prominently. It was an ugly face, bony, though young bony faces can be beautiful.

He took her to his car, unlocked the door from the sidewalk side and held it for her. When she got in with a shy thank-you, he shut the door and went around to the street side so he could get behind the wheel.

He drove towards the West Side. He knew a pier which was shut this time of year. He had his plan all worked out.

They went under the highway. He remained silent, letting her study him, make the first move. "My, what a strong fellow you are." She was still smiling, still a bit shy. "You're so strong and young." She bent forward and squeezed his knee.

He was surprised at her boldness. He smiled.

"Where are we going?"

He didn't mince words. "To my place, but first I have to stop at one of these piers. That's why we're going under and not over the West Side Drive."

"Why do we have to stop at one of the piers?"

"I'm the manager of this pier for two shipping firms. I have to stop to get two or three things at the office." He smiled and looked sideways. "You don't mind?"

She waved a palm at him. "No, no, go right ahead." Again she bent forward with a smile and squeezed his knee.

The old bitch, he thought to himself, hoping she would not go any further up his leg. The drive would not be long. He smiled at her and received a beaming smile in return.

What she'll get will surprise her, he mused to himself. Then he said, "Would you like to see where I work?"

"Oh, yes. Are there many people there?"

"Today it's closed. Some crazy holiday, I don't know which. Anyhow, I was going to stop off at the office, but I decided to stop for a drink first. Lucky I did."

"So no one's in the office. You sly devil. What are you

going to do? Are you going to put me down on one of the desks?"

"Oh, Madam, nothing so crude."

"Be crude, be crude," she urged breathlessly. He threw back his head and laughed. In a minute they came to the pier. As he expected, it was deserted.

"Come, we'll go around the outer edge. The office is in back, up a flight of stairs, facing the sea. The owners like it better."

He put an arm around her shoulders. It was so smooth and quick that she was startled for a second. She stopped, he looked at her and she smiled, sure of herself now.

She looked at him, confused. "Where are the signs for your shipping firm?"

"The signs? Up high on the wall. You have to look up. Tilt your head back."

"And the office?"

"The signs first, Connie." He pointed up at the wall. "Look up." She began looking, craning her neck from one side to the other.

"Where?" she asked, her neck stretched taut, the wrinkles and lines now deep grooves in the skin.

"The signs, my dear, are in your mind." She was about to look down when his hands clenched her throat and squeezed hard. Her head came down and to the side. Her mouth was open, twisted, her eyes bulged, not so much with the force of strangulation, as with the shock of what she had walked into.

He squeezed hard and felt her neck giving way. Her breath hit him, a sharp mixture of whiskey and tobacco. Her hands clawed his, her fingernails then raked down the backs, leaving long tatters of skin that soon filled with blood. Small droplets ran down his hands and along his wrists, and dripped onto the concrete below them.

He could not get her hands off his, that would mean letting go of her neck. He looked away from her. She tried to kick him in the shins, weakly. She wasn't a strong woman and even seized by death, she could not stay the hand of the executioner.

Marlin looked out across the blue-black, choppy water of the Hudson. Sweat started out at his hairline and ran down his forehead. One drop ran into his eye. It was salty, smarted. He closed the eye and squeezed harder.

A tug was moving up river. He pulled her closer to him so the men on the tug might think it was a couple embracing. His hold did not slacken as the tug came by.

It boomed a few times and then was hundreds of feet away. He felt her lose consciousness. Few people realize how long it takes to strangle someone. Marlin was learning how tiring it was. In his career he had strangled three people, and all of them with rope, never with his bare hands.

It was harder this way, but it had happened so suddenly. This had been opportunity itself. She had come to him, not the other way around.

Once she lost consciousness she dropped in his hands like a heavy weight. He struggled to hold her up, breathing hard. Then she urinated and the ammonia smell was thick in the air, she defecated and the smell of shit mingled with the urine smell. He tried holding his breath but it was impossible.

Marlin let go of her neck. His fingermarks were thick on her pale skin. Her face was blue-red, mottled, her tongue lolled, her eyes were open, bulging at him accusingly.

He looked around. No one. He picked her up again and struggled to the edge of the pier. She was dead weight now. He could not believe a woman so frail-looking could be so heavy.

At the edge he dropped her, then used his feet to kick her over. She went with a splash, water droplets splattered him. A small froth of bubbles filled the circle of rippling water where she had gone under.

Marlin looked down at the bloody trails on the backs of his hands. This had never happened. He looked back where she had lain. A puddle of urine marked the spot. Suddenly, for the first time in a very long time, he felt sick.

Chapter Sixteen

Marlin found a washroom where he could clean up, then stopped in a drug store to buy bandages. Though he kept one hand in his pocket, he had to bring the other out to pay. The druggist saw his hand and gave him a strange look but was silent.

Marlin put the bandages on his hands in the car. He should have bought something to put on so he wouldn't get any infection.

On second thought he drove to a gas station with an outside booth, put a dime into the phone and dialed

Purcell's number.

He recognized the voice the second Purcell picked up the phone and said, "Hello?"

"Mike here. Good news. Your wife is no more."

"What?"

"You heard."

"But how, Mike? How so quick?"

"Opportunity itself. I followed her to a movie, waited till she got out and followed her again. She went to a bar to have a drink."

"Adelaide? You're mistaken. Adelaide never drinks." Purcell realized his mistake in tense. "I mean she never drank."

"That's one more thing you never knew about her. She drank, and she liked to pick up younger men."

"You shock me." It seemed strange to Marlin that Purcell should be more shocked by her behavior than by her death.

"I'll shock you some more. She picked me up. She thought she was going to my apartment. She went someplace else instead."

Purcell didn't ask where. A bit more sober and believing, he said, "So she picked you up."

"Right. I figured it was opportunity itself. Instead of going around looking for her and for a right time, I figured this was the right time and it turned out to be."

"I see what you mean. How did she die?" Marlin went into a short account of why he never told his client how his wife had perished. Purcell understood and did not press the matter, which was good.

"When do I pay you the money?"

"Tomorrow. Don't go in to work. Meet me."

"Where and when?"

"I haven't decided. I'll give you a call. Be at your phone

at nine sharp." Before Purcell could say more he heard the click of the phone being hung up then the dial tone.

He put the phone back in its cradle.

Marlin returned to his hotel a bit late. He was tired, edgy. When he opened the door he heard a giggle. Lilly was standing there. His attache case was open and money was spread all over the bed. She held a fistful and had obviously been counting it when he came in.

Stunned, he stepped into the room and shut the door hard so it rattled in the frame. He looked back. Easy, boy. No noise. You'll draw attention.

Things were closing in too fast. He stood there a second, then said, "What's this?"

"Money," she said, letting a rain of fifties fall down. "Mind if I have some?" When he said nothing she added, "You're not what you claim to be."

"Few people are. What do you think I am?" His voice was tight and calm. He waited for her answer. The fun and games were over. They would never screw again, he knew.

She pointed playfully at him, still not aware of what she had done. "You're a bank robber." He smiled, going to her slowly and taking the bills she held.

He threw them on the bed with the rest. "You're wrong. I'll let you have another guess, but first let me get you a drink."

"Sure, sweetie." As he walked away, she said, "It certainly was lucky, me finding you. Not only are you a good lover, and young and nice to talk to, but you have money. You have no idea what a hard thing it is for a girl to find those combinations in a man. Usually guys with bread are old and lousy in bed."

He picked up a suitcase standing at the foot of his bed and put it on the bed. Deftly, he opened it and rummaged about under his shirts. He found the metal cylinder, removed it and walked back to her.

She looked at the can he held, then pointed. "That's Drano. What kind of cocktail is that?"

"What kind of reception is this?" He pointed to the money on the bed and floor. "Is this what a guy's girl does when he's away?"

She felt ashamed and looked down. Still thinking he was joking, she said, "I wanted to see how you lived. I was only here once. You've been to my place many times. I like you and want to know more about you." She began to pout, but he told her to stop it. The edge in his voice made her cease.

"How did you get in?"

"The edge of a credit card. I used it to slip the lock." Proud of herself, she said with a smile, "It's a trick my daddy taught me."

"I'll bet." Then he stopped. This was enough talking. He had things to do and there wasn't time to play with this vixen. His face set into a mask.

He advanced on her. She tried to run past him, but a balled fist caught her in the neck. She staggered back, lost her balance and fell on the bed.

When she rose and made a run for the door, he kicked her hard in the belly. She doubled over and stayed that way, gasping for air.

He pulled the top off the can of Drano, grabbed her by the hair and pulled her head up and back. She was paralyzed from the blow.

Her wide-open, fearful eyes stared at him in shock. She was paralyzed by the jolt, unable to speak, but words began to form and traveled up her throat.

He jammed the open end of the can into her mouth and rammed it in hard. She changed color, her face grew very red. Her mouth did fantastic gyrations around the can. She grabbed at the hand holding the can, but it did not move. She tried to pull away, but he held her hair so tight, the skin was being pulled up away from the skull, some strands of hair even came loose.

As the Drano ran down her throat to her stomach, he said, "Drink, drink, my love," through clenched teeth and held on. She wiggled like a worm on a hook and he thought of Adelaide Purcell and smiled. This one, too, tried to kick him, but the kick was feeble.

The Drano was almost empty. He took it from her mouth, which was bloody because he had bruised her gums and the tip of her tongue had got caught between her teeth and the edge of the can.

He threw the Drano on the floor. Her mouth smelled of chemicals and he let her drop. Her face was already blue, and though she twitched, it was not much. He got a newspaper, opened it wide and put it under her head.

A Drano kill was one of the methods he had used in the past and he always carried a few cans with him wherever he went. He put the newspaper under her head because sometimes victims vomited before dying, and he didn't want stains on the carpet.

He watched as one final spasm traveled up and down her body. A spurt of yellowish vomit mixed with blood was ejected from her mouth, staining her face and the paper under her. It was followed by a second spurt and then she stopped twitching.

Her face was mottled black and white now. He bent down and slipped the paper from under her, used it to wipe her face, and bunched it up and put it in a corner. He would dispose of it later.

Marlin went to his door, opened it slowly and looked out into the hall. It was empty. He went to her, felt along her body for her keys, found them and slipped out of his room. He went to her door, unlocked it, looked back around the hall and slipped inside.

He went out immediately, leaving the door a tiny bit ajar, and returned to his room. Putting her keys in his pocket, he bent and hoisted her over his shoulder.

Going to his door, he listened for sounds in the hall beyond. Nothing. If luck was with him, no one would come suddenly out of a room and see them.

Opening his door with one hand, he slipped out into the hall. He stopped to shut the door and went down the hall as fast as possible to her door. He was breathing fast, the strain of her weight too much for him. He was out of shape.

He came to her door, kicked it open with his foot and went inside. He dropped her on the floor and shut the door. Dropping her wasn't so smart, he realized. Someone below might complain to the management.

He went back to the door and looked out into the hall. Still no one. Then he returned to his room and sat down on his bed a second to think.

Getting her body out of the hotel was impossible, so he would have to get out. The police would come and pick up prints. They'd send them to Washington and soon they would know that a man who called himself Mike Bohenka was really Mike Marlin, and that possibly he had killed her.

His picture, general features and prints would be circulated throughout the city and he would have to watch himself. To think that after all these years he had got in trouble, all because of a cheap go-go dancer he should never have gone near in the first place.

He had disobeyed his own rule of never socializing with a woman on his home base while on a job, and it had hurt him. He thought for a second of cleaning up his prints, but there was no way of remembering every place he had touched over a period of days.

Marlin would just disappear and forget it. That was the only way. The picture the cops would get would do them little good. It was badly taken and more than a decade old.

He would pack, then go. It did not take long. He picked up his phone and called the desk. "This is Mr. Bohenka. I'm leaving. Could you make up my bill?"

"But Mr. Bohenka, I thought you were staying with us a few more weeks."

"I was going to, but something came up. I'll be leaving town."

"All right, we'll have your bill ready."

Chapter Seventeen

Ryker got what he wanted. Essex got bail from Judge Hollister. Ryker cursed the judge when he found that all he asked was fifteen thousand.

MacKenzie, the newest man on the homicide squad, was given the job of tracking Essex. He spent the day following him to his lawyer's office, his own office and home. That night he went home and an hour later emerged, walked two blocks to a parking lot, got his car and drove to his girl's house.

She was a pert blonde, a nice dresser. He took her to a

good restaurant near LaGuardia and then back to his apartment. MacKenzie was replaced at two in the morning by a man named Dusty Halloran.

He kept the shift until noon. By that time he had followed Essex to the girl's house, where he dropped her off, then to his office and at noon to a restaurant about three blocks away, where he was relieved by MacKenzie again.

MacKenzie watched Essex leave the restaurant, go to a phone booth and make a call. Then he went to sit in his car in the lot in front of the restaurant.

It wasn't a long wait. After twenty minutes a gray Plymouth pulled into the lot. A tall man in a brown wool jacket got out. He looked around the lot, sighted Essex and waved, but Essex did not see him. He was looking straight ahead, nervously smoking a cigarette.

The man went over to the car and knocked on the window. Essex was startled, craned his head sharply to the left. When he saw who it was, he smiled weakly, opened the door and slid across the seat.

MacKenzie had his pad out and had written down the license number of the gray Plymouth. He also noted the features of the stocky man who had driven the car into the lot.

Presently the man got out of Essex's car and Essex slid back behind the wheel. The other man held the door open and bent over as he spoke to Essex, who had his head tilted up to catch every word.

They shook hands and the man left. Essex closed his door and started his car. The man got back into the Plymouth, and started out of the lot in a puff of white exhaust.

When he drove off MacKenzie was on his trail. When they got to a main thoroughfare, he lost him, but that didn't matter too much. He had the license, assuming it was real.

He returned to the precinct with the information. Ryker had it checked with the State Bureau of Motor Vehicles. In an hour they had the name and address of their man.

His home address was in Rego Park, and his name was Steven Wunch. His occupation was listed as broker. He arranged sales of stores to prospective customers and specialized in groceries. A check with New York C.I.D showed he was a bookie with an operation that stretched across northern Queens and parts of Brooklyn. He had an arrest record dating back to 1941.

"Have him followed. I want to know every move he makes," Fischetti told the men under him. "That bastard's going to go someplace today or tomorrow, and I want to know where."

Two hours after Wunch had left Essex, plainclothes police in unmarked cars were shadowing his home and business office, and his phones had been tapped.

Steven Wunch picked up his phone, dialed a number he never wrote down, only kept in his head. "This is Wings. Tell Almore I've got to see him."

Tony DeTorio, older than he had been in Miami, got on the line. "I hear you want to talk to me."

"Not over the phone. Someone might be listening. This is about a mutual friend. I'd like to talk it over."

"Let's meet in about an hour, on a bench in Prospect Park."

"The regular one?"

"Yeah."

"I'll be seeing you," Wunch said, then hung up.

The police were already tapping every line running into Wunch's office and heard the conversation. They had a van with a special boom bug ready to go whenever Wunch left for Prospect Park.

This boom bug was like a long finger that could be pointed in the direction of the speakers and pick up even whispers in the midst of heavy noise at distances of up to one hundred yards.

Wunch met DeTorio as promised and they got down to business right away. Wunch told how Essex had come to him complaining about his police trouble. He explained Essex wanted him to tell the police that the twenty thousand was paid to him.

"Don't be a fool. You can't save this Essex," DeTorio warned. "He's a goner. If you came forward you'd just go to jail and have to pay taxes on twenty grand you never got."

"I know. He's willing to pay," Wunch explained, "but I'm not game. That isn't the thing. If he cracks, my ass is flame."

"I understand, I understand," DeTorio said. "Essex will have to go. If they know about him and the other guys, then Mike is in trouble and so am I. We'll have to tell Mike so he can knock these people off. This can't go on. They'll get Mike, then they'll get me.

"I served time in Florida once with Mike. I don't want to any more. That was the last rap for me. Now that I'm up north, I keep my nose clean."

"Look, DeTorio. I know all about you and Guiteau. That isn't what counts. We got to get Essex off my back. Call Mike. Tell him the score and have him pick the time and place. These hits will have to be free. For me, for you, and for his own sake too."

DeTorio rubbed his chin. "Don't know where he is. He didn't leave any address with me. From time to time he calls. When he does, I'll tell him what gives and he'll take care of it. I've known Mike a long time. He can be depended on."

"I certainly hope so," Wunch said. He didn't sound too happy.

Marlin looked over his new hotel room. He had taken a room high up in the Dixie Hotel, overlooking the west Forties, just off Times Square.

He sat down on his bed and smoked a cigarette and thought about Lilly. They wouldn't miss her for at least a day. When she didn't show up at work, her employer would call the hotel and they would buzz her room. There would be no answer and the desk would tell her boss she wasn't in.

Tomorrow morning the cleaning woman would come around and knock, and when there was no answer she would unlock the door and step inside. But Marlin was safe.

It would take the police a while to get a make on him; and they certainly wouldn't think of looking in another hotel like this. They would assume he had left the city all together. He smiled and continued smoking his cigarette.

DeTorio returned to his apartment on the Upper West Side. He called LaRue Guiteau, but no one answered.

Guiteau and DeTorio had come to New York five years ago and established themselves here. They had not known of Marlin's whereabouts and he had not known of theirs till he came to New York and needed people to connect him with husbands who wanted their wives out of the way.

As soon as Guiteau heard about the new killer in town, the one with the strange preference, he knew it had to be Marlin. The reunion between them was a night to remember, as they went to fancy restaurants and spent the night with some of the best call girls in town.

Now this. DeTorio tried his friend's number again. There

was an answer this time. DeTorio told Guiteau the whole sad tale. "Oh, my God," the other answered. "We have to do something."

"Has Marlin called?"

"Not yet. I haven't heard from him in a few days. He should call. Then again, that's only if he wants to go out for a night on the town. I expect he's been working hard and will be wanting to. But if he wants jobs, he'll call Poagie Reeves. Poagie does that sort of thing here. He just collects the information from guys like us, but he himself is the funnel."

"Then call Poagie and tell him we want him to give Marlin a message. Hear me?"

"Will do."

Ryker and Fischetti sat around looking over the information they had. Lindly was out for coffee again. Myers, one of the detectives at the next row of desks, came by and dropped a list of yesterday's murders on Ryker's desk.

There was nothing for Ryker. He threw the sheet to the side and read the results so far in the case, then looked up.

"Essex goes to his bookie like I expected. His bookie goes to meet a man in Prospect Park. The man's name is DeTorio. I'm going to run a check on all the DeTorio's we know in this city and anyone named Guiteau and some guy Mike they spent time with in a Florida pen. This Mike is the hit man. Mike who?"

"Get the killer and you'll know," Fischetti said.

"Very funny, Sal. You know, thinking about this, I find it funny that all those killed were women, and married women at that. About two years ago this same thing happened. There was a whole spate of killings like that, in fact."

Fischetti snapped his fingers. "Yeah, I should've remembered earlier. There's this hit man who kills only wives. The Wife Killer, they call him. He hits all over the U.S. Stays a few months then whizzes off to do his work elswhere."

"Think this is him?" Ryker asked.

"I have a strong suspicion it may be. He's an experienced bird and if we get him, we'll be getting someone who's been around a long, long time."

"How come they never caught him, Sal?"

"Bad technique. They'd suspect a few husbands, pull them in and ask questions, but by then he was gone. We didn't do that. We made a pigeon sweat, so he'd run to his bookie, who would lead us to the next man in line and so on. We could have made our pigeon talk and then gone to the bookie, who'd clam up and there it would have ended. Those boys aren't known for talking."

"Word would have got to this Mike," Ryker cut in. "He would've gone away and emerged someplace else in another disguise, with a whole new identity. You know how these boys operate. They buy new identities the way you and I buy cigars. It's the mob that's behind them there."

"Let's hope we're playing this right, Joe."

"We are. I have a gut feeling." Then he added, "the more you look at this case, the more little helpful details emerge to help us."

Chapter Eighteen

Nothing happened the rest of that day. Marlin emerged only to eat supper. Essex went home and stayed there. The other two husbands spent uneventful days at home. DeTorio, who had been followed, and Guiteau spent the evening at the Riverboat Restaurant.

Ryker returned home and spent the evening watching TV and reading magazines. He found both activities boring and uneventful. It wasn't until the next day that the wheels began to turn.

Marcel was able to get rid of his wife's relatives. Alone

for the first time in days, he dialed Sylvie and told her not to go to work that day. He was coming to her house.

She was reluctant to stay home, but he persuaded her. Sylvie rushed her boy friend out of the house and cleaned things up for Marcel's visit.

He came, wearing a new suit, carrying flowers and a bottle of champagne. Her annoyance vanished when she saw him. She invited him in, they kissed, she found goblets for the champagne. They toasted each other, and exchanged pleasantries. She asked about his period of mourning and he told her in a few words about the highlights. Then she asked when they were going to release his wife.

"The police say tomorrow. I'll have to arrange a funeral."

"Did they find the killer, or are they on his trail?" she wanted to know.

"Not yet, and I don't think they will find him. It was that kind of murder."

She wanted to ask more, but he hushed her. "I'm not here to speak about the dead, darling, but about the living. You and me."

She played with her goblet. "Please don't say that, Eddie. I'm fond of you, very fond, but not ready for marriage."

He was angry and wanted to say, you're no spring chicken, what are you waiting for? Instead he suggested, "Why don't you start thinking in that direction? There's no time like the present. There'll be no better opportunity."

"I don't know, Eddie." What would he say to the man she had been living with?

"Look at me, Sylvie. I'm still young and vigorous. Soon I'll be burying a bitch. No, don't say anything, she was a bitch and may she rot in hell for the years I suffered with her. You were my only solace then, and still are. You are my hope for the future."

"I'm still fairly young. I make a good living, Sylvie, almost a hundred thousand a year. Sylvie, we can go places, do things. We can see Paris in the summer, Acapulco in the autumn, Miami in winter. Have you ever seen waves so big they bowl you over?" His eyes glimmered.

"No, I haven't."

"There's a beach north of Miami I could take you to, a beauty of a place. Oh, Sylvie, the world is waiting for us. Don't say no, honey. Don't say no."

She walked away from him and sat on the couch, placing the champagne goblet on the coffee table. "I don't know, Eddie." Suddenly when he put it that way all the world seemed her oyster. It didn't always have to be Ralph. He was younger, but it could still be good with Eddie. He wasn't so bad in the sack, and he had so much more than Ralph to offer. What did Ralph make? Two hundred a week? He wasn't the opportunity of a lifetime.

How many times did a girl have an opportunity to marry a well-off man? Not every day, of that she was certain. Her mother would call her a fool for refusing. She was weakening, she looked to him with pleading eyes for an answer. He came to her, sat beside her.

He began to kiss her and she didn't resist. Then he rose and took her by the hand, urged her towards the bedroom. She did not resist his pull.

Much later they emerged from her house hand in hand. He walked towards his car. There was a distant fire in his eyes, smothered a bit by love making.

He stood with her near his car, kissed her once on the lips, and said, "I'll have to stop in at the office for a few hours to see how business is going. Tonight I'll be by again." She wanted to say no, even started to, but stopped.

She was worried about Ralph, but she could handle him.

Marcel wanted to say more when two men came up the sidewalk and stopped. "You're Mr. Marcel?"

Too confused to say nything, he nodded. They showed him badges. "We'd like you to come down to headquarters with us. Sergeant Ryker wants to speak with you."

The officer looked at Sylvie and smiled. "I hope you don't mind, ma'am." She shook her head, speechless.

The policeman said, "You won't need your car, Mr. Marcel. Come in ours. This way, please." Marcel went numbly, not even saying goodbye to Sylvie.

How had they found him? They followed him, of course. But why? Maybe they suspected about him and Marlin?

Sylvie followed them with her eyes, wondering what this was all about.

The maid unlocked the door of Lilly's room, after knocking six times and getting no answer. She recoiled, grabbed her face and screamed. The two maids down the hall came running.

She pointed in horror at the body. In death she rested as she had fallen. After-death spasms had induced another round of vomiting and now her vomit-covered face and chest drew their gaze. The room smelled foul.

One of the maids ran down the hall. "I'm going to call Mr. McCarren. He's got to see this."

The other two shut the door and stood in the hall, bent towards each other, their eyes fearful and confused. This was a matter for the police. Murder, for sure.

Ryker came in early that day. He had asked that Essex, Wilcox and Marcel be brought in. They weren't going to be targets for any hit man. Besides, they'd make good witnesses after they talked, and talk they would, eventually. Protective custody wouldn't hurt them any. He'd talked it over with Fischetti and Deputy Inspector Connolly and both men had agreed.

At eleven in the morning the police barge fished up the body of an older, gray-haired woman, fully dressed. She had been strangled. She was taken to Bellevue, prepared for autopsy and fingerprinted. The prints were checked and happened to be on file.

When Adelaide Purcell was twenty-nine years old, she had gone to work as a typist in a government office and there was printed. Her name and various facts came in.

The sheet with the murders for the day did not come across Ryker's desk till five, just before he would normally go home. He had stayed overtime, and set it aside.

For now, Ryker had other things on his mind. He needed to find out where DeTorio and Guiteau would go, but first Mike had to call them.

A quick check of their names on police department rap sheets showed two DeTorios, only one Tony DeTorio and a LaRue Guiteau, the only man with that name. This report came in at eleven.

Ryker brought it in to Fischetti, called Lindly in and together they looked over the reports on the two men. They hadn't been arrested in New York, but their sheets were extensive.

They were suspected of having dealt in drugs, stolen Cadillacs, hot rocks, illegal gold and furs. Also they had a lucrative sideline of getting hit men in and out of cities, and they had connections with all the right people.

Fischetti put the report down. "There's more on these birds. We need their Florida record. Check on the prison they were sent to. Find out who the third guy sent up with them was. His first name is Mike. Get his prints in here, anything you can, Joe. Find me anyone in the city they deal with, then go visit them. Do it fast, this is building. The bird we want may fly the coop, then all this will have been for nothing."

Ryker nodded. "You want it, you got it. Just let me at this and I'll go through it faster than a hungry hound."

"You do that, Joe." Fischetti tapped him fondly on the shoulder. Ryker smiled. "I'll make you proud, dad," he joked.

"Get the hell out of here," Fischetti snarled. "Bring back the gold, Joe."

"I will." They rose and shook hands.

Marlin met Purcell, got his money as planned, and bid him goodbye and good luck on his new life. Then he returned to his room. Not bad pay for two days' work.

He should go see Poagy. Poagy would be nervous about his cut. With that in mind, Marlin counted out four thousand in fifties, stuffed it into his pocket, locked up his room and went to Poagie's office.

It was on the ground floor of a west Forties tenement not far from the river, in a storefront that had a coat of paint over the windows.

The front room was full of folding chairs. You had to go down a long hall with peeling walls, roaches on the ceiling and under foot, then you reached a long, bare room with wooden floors, holes in the wall, two bare bulbs hanging from the ceiling by long insulated wires and below them a folding table and chairs. On one of those chairs sat Poagy Reeves.

He looked up at Marlin, the cigar in his jowled mouth dropping thirty degrees. He put down the cards he held, so surprised he almost put them down face up.

The other men at the table also put their cards down, rose and stepped against the walls.

"Got a present for you, Poagy." Marlin took the four thousand out, threw it on the table. Poagy's eyes dropped to the money, then glued themselves to Marlin's face again.

He was calm now. Even his cigar did not move. He spoke around it. "Thanks. Everything okay?"

"Nice. Not bad. Got any more jobs?"

Poagy shook his head. "Not so far." He looked back at the money. "How much there?"

"Four gees."

"I owe forty percent to your friends. DeTorio gets twenty and Guiteau another twenty percent. Not bad for a little work. You could've gone to them straight."

"I didn't know about it. I asked around and was told you were the man to see."

"Well, you don't have to no more. You can deal through them two."

"How come you're so generous? That cuts you out of twelve hundred each time some broad gets chopped."

"I ain't generous, no way. I just been asked by the boys to do this, on account of they're your pals. For anyone else, I'd do the dealing."

"It's nice of them to think of it after I've done four kills and paid out thousands I didn't have to. Some pals."

Poagy took the cigar out of his mouth and motioned to the wall behind him. "Talk to them about it." Marlin nodded.

He turned to leave. "One more thing, Mike. They want to talk to you urgent. They passed the word to me in case I see you. Contact them."

"Why?"

Poagy shrugged. "They didn't say, Mike. You know how it is."

"Thanks." Marlin turned around and walked out. There wasn't a sound except for his feet along the wooden flooring.

Cilhooley, the detective who came up to arrange the removal of Lill's body and talk to the owner of the place where she worked was now talking to the desk man.

"You say you saw her yesterday, around two in the afternoon?"

"That's right," he answered. "Two o'clock, a little before."

"Any friends here that you know of?" The clerk shook his head.

"What about the people around her, on both sides of the hall?"

"Maybe Mr. Bohenka. He was young, kind of good looking."

"Can I speak with him?"

"I'm sorry, he checked out kind of suddenly yesterday. He said something had come up." As soon as he said it the clerk knew it sounded bad, so did Gilhooley. He began to ask about Bokenka and asked to see his room. The desk clerk went to get the keys.

Ryker had a report on a certain Poagy Reeves, con man, fixer, taker of things, fence, a man with a gimmick for those on the lam and in need of a place to stay, suspected contact man for hit men.

Ryker found out what pen the boys had spent time in. He called long distance, got the warden, identified himself, gave him the specifics of the case, said he needed the information fast, wanted it over the wire. He couldn't wait till the mail brought it up.

The warden understood. He asked Ryker to give him a half hour, so he could have one of his men look the information up and then call Ryker.

Ryker hadn't had lunch yet though it was past two. He waited and the call was returned. It was being handled now by Assistant Warden Kent Ames.

Ames told him of the three men that had been sent to their prison and the crimes for which they had been sent up. He then read off the names and the sentences and when each man was paroled.

Michael G. Martin was the name Ryker wanted. He was smiling when he hung up and walked into Fischetti's office. The lieutenant had gone to lunch, so he found Lindly and told him what he had.

Lindly shrugged. "All you have is a name. The guy is probably using an alias, he'd be stupid not to. Names aren't everything. You have to find the man behind the name."

"That I will," Ryker said and walked away. Now that he had a name he had a chance of checking on identity. He contacted Washington and asked that Mike Martin's prints be sent to New York immediately. He explained what crime Martin had been incarcerated for, when the prints had been taken and why they were needed.

They were wired to him and by a quarter to four information was piling up. Fischetti was back from lunch then. Ryker brought him what he had so far.

"Good, keep it up. MacKenzie is still sitting outside DeTorio's house and Parker is sitting outside Guiteau's. Nothing on either man so far. Martin hasn't contacted them."

"Do you want to talk to Essex, Wilcox and Marcel?"

"Let them sit and stew a few hours. Then we'll bring them into the conference room together. I want them to see each other. The effect of seeing so many men being discovered at once, all connected to the same killer might induce at least one to talk, try to make a deal."

"Could be," Fischetti added. "Keep working on what

you have."

Detective Sergeant Gilhooley had the fingerprint men go through the empty room Marlin had left behind. He had a strong suspicion of who had murdered the go-go dancer. Prolonged questioning of various hotel workers and some of the people on the floor brought forth a few who admitted seeing Marlin taking Lilly out. Gilhooley had a link. By the time the body was taken to the ambulance outside, the print men had done their job and the prints were rushed to the lab to be checked.

They didn't have to wait for Adelaide Purcell's prints to come back from Washington. An attendant outside the autopsy room was going through her clothes and found a waterlogged folded slip that had been missed in one of her pockets.

It was made out to her, giving her name and address and the address of the dry cleaning establishment where she had left some clothes. It was a signed bill with everything itemized.

The attendant showed it to the doctor in charge, who called the police. They took the slip, thanked the careful attendant and made a call to Wilbur Purcell. He wasn't home. He had gone out to celebrate, perhaps a bit prematurely.

Her name went on the list of those murdered and was sent around to each precinct. Next to her name was the sentence: Murder Unsolved.

When Ryker saw it, he almost went by it, but came back. Only one other woman had been murdered in New York City that day, and her common-law husband had given himself up two hours earlier. Crime Solved was printed next to this one. But this Adelaide Purcell seemed different. She was past middle age, just in the right range. Something told Ryker he should look into this. He told Lindly to check with the precinct the report had originated from.

Marlin did not feel like talking to his old friends. He was mad at them for having cost him so many extra dollars when he didn't have to pay them in the first place. He had assumed without asking that they worked it as they did because that was the way the local mob wanted it, and after years in the business he did very little asking.

It had been a low risk operation and they had treated him like dirt. He didn't waste time moping about it. He called a local whore agency. For seventy-five dollars they sent over a decent girl and you could spend a few hours nicely. He called them and gave his hotel and room nunber. He had used their service a few weeks ago and they remembered him or seemed to, after a short pause to consult their book.

"You've changed your hotel," the harsh-voiced woman said. "Yeah," he answered, and asked when the girl would be over.

"Half an hour," he was told. The whore business was a good business, he thought. Seventy-five was plenty for a girl who wasn't really that good.

Ryker found no one could contact Purcell. He went to see Fischetti and asked that a financial check of Wilbur Purcell be made.

"What's he do for a living?"

"We've got his name and address. Check it with the banking community. They'll give you his occupation and everything. In particular, I want to know what withdrawals he's made this past week."

"Okay, Joe, we'll check. But I think you're carrying this a bit far. You've got the whole damn city being checked. This guy is a hit man, not God. He can't be killing every woman around the area."

"Not every woman, Sal. Just these women."

Fischetti made a weary motion with his hand, then said, "I'll check for you."

"Listen to me, Sal. If this is the man I think it is, we can get our hands on the worst uncaged hit man in this country. I've been checking the file on this wife killer. I called the Central Intelligence Division and asked for a rundown. They tell me this guy is suspected of having killed over three hundred people in a career spanning more than twenty years.

"He's an underground legend, a faceless killer wanted by the police department of every major city. But now he's unmasked. We know his name, we have his prints and I'm going to try to get his picture by wirephoto from the Florida office that has his mug shots."

"It's too late today," Fischetti reminded him.

"I know, but tomorrow is another day and after that there'll be one more. We've got him. He doesn't know it yet, but we've got him pegged. All that remains is the roundup."

"Good luck," Fischetti said, still skeptical.

Chapter Nineteen

It was a windy, rainy day, but Gilhooley came in early and went to the lab section to get the fingerprint reports. The print men had separated twelve perfect samples of what they regarded to be Bohenka's prints. Sent to Washington, they were returned with a rap sheet on a certain Michael G. Martin, who had spent time in a Florida pen in the late fifties.

This information went out on the police teletype. All cars were alerted to look for the man. A wirephoto was sent to Gilhooley's precinct and from there copies were later made and sent to all Manhattan precincts.

It was just after one when the Twenty-First Precinct got the sheet. Lindly noticed it first and brought it in to Ryker. "Look at this. Martin killed a girl named Lilly Barron in a residency hotel over on Ninth Avenue."

"Let me see that." Ryker read it over. "Get me Gilhooley's number. I want to talk to him. No, wait, you talk to him, find out all he knows. I'm going over to C.I.D. headquarters to see the file on Martin. I want to see the police drawing of him that they have. Also, see if Gilhooley has a composite drawing on Martin yet."

Before Lindly could answer, Ryker had his trench coat on and was gone. Lindly scratched his head and went to do what Ryker had asked.

Marlin slept late that day. He got up and went out for a late breakfast-lunch at a steak house. The food wasn't bad and not expensive.

Then he stepped into a nearby theater to see a sex picture for three dollars. The show would last three hours, so at least the early afternoon would be killed.

When he finally got out he was in a better mood, less mad at DeTorio and Guiteau for what they had done. He was seriously thinking of ggiving them a call.

Ryker returned from C.I.D. headquarters and asked for Lindly. He was told Lindly had left with Sergeant Gilhooley. They were going to the residency hotel to interview some people.

Ryker went to see Sal Fischetti. "I've got the goods for you. Our pigeon has a career that stretches way back to 1947. The F.B.I. has hunted him on and off for years without luck. They have no photos, only a composite drawing."

Ryker threw a faded post office poster on Fischetti's desk. The poster gave descriptions of Martin, or Marlin, and a brief history of his criminal life. Ryker and Fischetti read it over.

"The F.B.I. has looked for Marlin at varying periods," Ryker commented. "Over the years through name changes, changes in address and modus operandi, he kept one or two steps ahead of the law."

Fischetti blew out a gust of air. "Quite a man. They had an idea of how he looked, but were always too far behind. He used new identities and moved around."

"So our man is named Mike Marlin, he served a term in a Florida pen and they never knew his real identity. But the term in the pen gave the authorities his prints. And now we have them here. All we need is the man that matches the prints and all will be well."

"Keep looking, Joe, keep looking."

"I will."

Lindly came back all excited. "Guess what, Joe?" Ryker wheeled around behind his desk. "I've been with Sergeant Jerome Gilhooley. He's got prints in, and guess who the man was who killed that go-go dancer? Mike Martin, the guy who served a term in Florida."

"Who's real name, according to the F.B.I., happens to be Michael Maximilian Marlitz," Ryker said. He changed it to Mike Marlin when he came into this country after the war. The Florida pen had him, and didn't know who they had.

"In a way this is good news. We know where our man was till two days ago. For all we know, he may have vanished into thin air. On the other hand, his method of operation would keep him around. He's a competent professional, a guy who's killed over three hundred people."

"How do you catch a man like that, Joe?"

"You just try hard. His luck has to give out some time, and it looks like this is the time. What's been happening lately does not augur well for him. What else did you get?"

"We went to interview the people in the hotel again. The clerk remembered Marlin receiving a call from a man called Poagie. Marlin wasn't in, but Poagie left a message to be called back. Marlin did. They routed the call through the switchboard. Unfortunately they don't remember the number any more. They put through many calls and don't keep records."

Ryker wasn't perturbed. He was thinking. "I've heard that name before." He turned and looked at the next desk, where detective Meyers was working.

"Hey, Meyers. Know any hood by the name of Poagie?"

Meyers tilted his head back. "I've heard that name a few times. Not in connection with homicide, but book-making. He has something to do with that. Let me make a call. I'll get you the dope." Meyers picked up the phone and began dialing.

Ryker rose, asked Lindly to come along and went to see if the information about Purcell had come in yet. His suspicions were confirmed. Purcell had taken twenty thousand from the bank also.

Ryker brought this to Fischetti. The minute the lieutenant saw it he gave orders that Purcell be brought in. When Ryker came back to his desk Meyer said, "Poagie is a fix-it man, who will put you in contact with anyone any time. That includes hit men. His full name is Poagie Reeves."

"And what's his address?" Ryker wanted to know. Meyers gave it to him. Ryker rose and said to Lindly, "Come on, we're picking this Poagie Reeves up."

"What for?" Lindly asked.

"Suspicion of gambling without a license. You have to have a license in this state to gamble. He doesn't, so we pick him up and bring him in. Then we bring him to the conference room where we will have Wilcox, Essex, Purcell and Marcel. The boys should be talking in a fairly short time."

"I'd like to be there," Lindly said.

"You will."

Reeves was shaken when they entered his storefront, marched to the back and kicked over the table full of cards, chips and bills. The cigar fell from Poagie's mouth, hit his fat belly and then the dirty wooden floor.

They flashed their badges and told him he was under arrest and the charge. While the others argued that the police had no right to do this, they frisked Poagie, found a knife, which they took, handcuffed him and led him out to their car.

The crowd grew less belligerent when they saw the two patrol cars full of uniformed police out front. Fischetti had arranged to have them come along when Ryker made his arrest.

Mike Marlin put a dime in the phone and dialed DeTorio's number.

"This is Mike. You want to see me, you son of a bitch?"

"Mike, Mike, where are you?"

"On the street."

"Well, dammit, come up, man. I have things to tell you. Tough things." The urgency in his voice told Marlin this was something serious. He had known DeTorio long enough.

Within twenty minutes he was in DeTorio's house. The men watching it saw Marlin, thought he pretty much fitted the description of the man they were looking for. They alerted an unmarked car to be ready to move out.

DeTorio offered him a drink. Marlin declined. "Where's LaRue?"

"Out lining up a few deals. It's not him we're here to talk about, but you. Things are beginning to come apart at the seams. The police have linked together three of the men you've done jobs for. They even have their bank statements showing that on the day after each murder these men took twenty thousand out of their account in cash.

"One of them, Essex, the first man you hit for, has been pulled in and told he'll be charged. He's out now on bail."

"That's bad." Marlin suddenly looked worried.

"That's not the half of it." DeTorio told him about the offer Essex had made his bookie.

"He'd be a fool to take him up," Marlin replied.

"Just what I said. You've got to hit these guys, Mike. For us, for you."

"Yeah, they'll talk when the police press down and now there's this new guy, Purcell. I strangled his wife and put her in the river. They should be fishing her out soon if they haven't already."

"Then you'll hit these guys? Shut them up before they talk. You've got to for us, for you." Marlin noted the concern on DeTorio's face.

"Not for me. I can be up and gone. These things have happened to me before, not so fast, though. They must be using a new technique, or else one hell of a team is working against me.

"If it was just for me, I'd get my bags packed and out of town. But there's other people, guys like you and LaRue. You did me wrong a few times, you cost me some money. I won't let that stand in my way, now when your necks are on the chopping block. I'll forget any differences I have for now and do these hits. The only thing I dislike is that it will have to be done for nothing."

"Sorry about that, Mike."

"Forget it, Tony." Marlin rose. "I'll be going now. I'll go to my hotel and plan this. These things can't be done on the spur of the moment, you know. Give my best to LaRue."

"I will, Mike."

When Marlin left a car was waiting. It followed him all the way to the Dixie. Two plainclothesmen went into the lobby, showed the manager their badges and asked to see him in his office. The lion had been tracked to his lair.

The wirephoto of Marlin came in. Ryker tacked it to the bulletin board at the side of the room and called all the detectives together.

"Come gather round. See the face that sank a thousand lives. This is the face you'll see in person here, today, if we're lucky."

"So this is Mike Marlin, the killer nobody could tag," Meyers said.

"Nobody till I came along," Ryker boasted.

"You haven't got him yet."

"I will, Meyers. Just wait and see. I'll show you poolroom sharpies what a real detective can do."

To the sound of their ribbing he walked away and told Lindly to get that fat Poagie Reeves up from the detention cell.

"Bring him to the reception room." When Lindly got there he found the four husbands sitting morosely, looking at one another. Ryker, Fischetti, Deputy Inspector Connolly, detective MacKenzie and a tape recorder, already on, completed the picture.

When Poagie Reeves walked into the room, the faces of

the four men fell. Poagie's face fell and Ryker beamed. He told Lindly to leave the door open. Lawyers for the suspected husbands had been called and would be here soon.

Ryker made Poagie sit near the husbands. He asked if Poagie wanted a lawyer. He did. "See anyone you like, Poagie?" The fat man didn't answer.

Poagie went out of the room to call his lawyer, and was escorted back in by the patrolman in the hall. The patrolman stood guard at the open door till the lawyers arrived.

Ryker disappeared and came back in a few minutes with Marlin's picture. "This was taken some years back, gentlemen, but I'm sure you'll recognize a close friend here. A man who has tinkered with fate.

"Soon we'll have him. If you boys know what's good for you you'll talk. It'll go easier with you later in court." The lawyers began to arrive and huddled with them in the far corners of the room, excited whispers passing to and fro.

Poagie Reeves would say nothing, but the lawyer for Essex wanted to make a deal. "My client will talk. He sees the situation is hopeless, I've advised him of that. He wishes to make a clean breast of it and throw himself on the mercy of the court."

Essex sat down at the table and began to tell his story from beginning to end as the tape recorder silently took down each word. He was barely done when Wilcox's lawyer indicated his client also wanted to confess. Marcel and Purcell were still holding back, but after Wilcox took his place and told his sad tale, implicating his bookie and Poagie Reeves, Marcel stepped forward.

Tears poured from his eyes as he told of years of anguish in his marriage and his final attempt to destroy the bane of his existence by hiring a hit man so he would be free to marry again. Between his tears he said he was glad he had done it.

Purcell still held back despite the desperate whispers of his lawyer. About Poagie Reeves there was no question. The sweating fat man would not tell. He was one man who had stayed alive so long because he told no tales. Now was not the time to break that perfect record.

In the middle of it all Meyers ran in. "They've found where Marlin is staying."

Ryker ran from the room, followed close by Lindly and Fischetti.

Chapter Twenty

Ryker had convinced them to keep the team small. Too many men would get in each other's way, fire a lot of unwarranted shots and perhaps kill innocent bystanders.

Connolly warned them to try and take him alive if possible.

Fischetti, Lindly and Ryker would go in first. All exits were covered. He could not get out. He could not fly away. Marlin was no bird. He was a man, a very vulnerable man, one who could be shot down. This was the end of the line for him.

DeTorio and Guiteau were picked up about then, as they walked out of DeTorio's apartment house. They were handcuffed, put in a waiting unmarked patrol car and driven off.

The three men picked for the assault went up in the elevator to the seventeenth floor, where Marlin had his room. Four uniformed patrolmen accompanied them, but got off at the sixteenth floor.

They would go to the fire stairs at either end of the hall and wait there to block any escape down the stairs by Marlin.

Ryker, Fischetti and Lindly had their guns out as they got out of the elevator and looked both ways down the hall. Two people were coming towards the elevator. One was a woman. She saw the trio with guns drawn and assumed they were bandits.

A scream escaped her mouth and she ran down the hall. The man saw them, and influenced by her scream, panicked and ran to his room. Several doors opened, heads poked out and then disappeared, doors slammed shut.

Marlin heard too. He jumped from the bed where he had been cleaning his gun and looked out. He understood then that these men had tracked him.

Quickly grabbing his attache case with the thirty-six thousand inside, he unlatched a suitcase, opened the attache case and shoveled thirty-six thousand more from the bottom of the suitcase into the attache case.

This seventy-two thousand dollars, his share of four hits, he locked in tight, opened his door and pulled a snub-nosed thirty-eight from the open suitcase. It they wanted him they would have to fight.

He waited behind the door. The three detectives approached cautiously. When they came to his door and saw it open, they were shocked. Had he gone?

Ryker went in first and stepped right into Marlin's trap. The minute he entered, Marlin smashed into the door. It flew outward, striking Ryker a hard blow and sending him reeling into the room. The other two were thrown back out.

Marlin ran towards Ryker and with all his might brought his gun butt down across the back of the detective's head. Ryker saw a white flash and partially lost consciousness. He still heard and felt things, but as if from the bottom of a deep black well.

Marlin grabbed the door and pulled inward, running back so he was behind it again. The two detectives outside did not charge in, but the open door provided a crack through which Marlin could see to shoot out into the hall while he hid behind the door.

He stuck his snub-nosed gun through and fired twice. One shot caught Fischetti in the thigh and toppled him, the other shot caught Lindly in the chest. He grimaced and crumpled, dropping his pistol.

Marlin pulled the door open and emerged. Fischetti was trying to aim his gun. Marlin struck him across the wrist with his pistol. The lieutenant dropped his weapon.

Marlin ran down the hall, attache case in hand. He reached the stairs and started down, then saw the patrolmen. They fired, he fired back and hit nothing.

Going on up, he headed toward the roof, then decided to go out on the eighteenth and top floor. He ran along the hall trying to get people to open their doors so he could hide in their rooms and outwit the police dragnet. No one would open. They had heard the shots.

Ryker stirred and rose. He took his gun and staggered into the hall. Fischetti lay there and so did Lindly. Lindly was white. There was blood on the cheap carpeting. "What happened?" he asked Fischetti.

"The bastard tricked us. He went to the stairs. Get him." Ryker nodded and ran. He got to the stairs and screamed down at the patrolmen on the floor below. "Where is he?"

"He went up, sir." Ryker hesitated and then went up. Marlin had no luck on the eighteenth floor and ran to the fire stairs at the other end, tried going down. Again a flurry of shots exploded. The patrolmen blocked him. They had orders not to go up, not to fall into any trap. They would leave the advancing to the detectives.

Ryker heard the shots and emerged on the eighteenth floor. He saw Marlin come out and fired a shot that buried itself in a wall. Trembling guests waited behind locked doors and listened to the firing.

Marlin retreated into the stairwell, his heart pounding. He went up to the roof.

He emerged on a small roof with a railing all around the outer edge. He hid behind a ventilation duct. Checking his pockets he saw he only had a few bullets. Quickly he ejected the spent shells and added the new ones. He didn't even have a full cylinder.

Ryker came up and waited. He didn't emerge, he would let Marlin sweat. If he had his other man they could have charged up from either stairwell, catching their man in front and back. But that wasn't possible. The two he had come up with would wind up in a hospital. He was alone and he would have to do this carefully.

After a few minutes Ryker took off his jacket and opening the door, hesitated a few seconds and tossed the jacket out. Marlin thought it was Ryker and, going for a quick kill so he could get the detective's gun and bullets, he fired a flurry of shots before he realized he'd been had. His gun was empty.

Ryker emerged onto the roof. He put his gun back in his holster. Connolly said he wanted him alive, and alive it would be.

"Come on, you bastard. This time you have to fight a man, no helpless woman. Come on." Ryker put his fists up. Marlin threw his gun.

Marlin wasn't scared. He threw the attache case. Ryker stepped to the side. The case glanced off his back and fell onto the tar paper roof. It hurt a bit, but not much.

Ryker rushed Marlin and the two were soon rolling around, Marlin trying to bite off Ryker's ear. But the tough detective didn't stand for that. He bit Marlin's nose. That made Marlin let go.

Getting to his feet he lifted Marlin up and slammed him in the face, belly, chest, kidneys. Marlin reeled, but recovered and kicked Ryker in the balls. Marlin slammed him in the side of the head and Ryker spit blood.

Marlin grabbed his attache case and ran to the stairs. Ryker limped after him, started to run and tackled Marlin. He went down, hit his mouth against the roof and began to bleed. Ryker pummeled him.

But Marlin slammed him over the head with his case and got up. He ran across the roof and almost made it to the other stairwell. Ryker was up, working on superhuman energy, ran into Marlin like a football player.

The other reeled, but regained his balance and aimed another kick at Ryker. He struck him again in the crotch. Ryker yelled. He forced himself to stand straight and through gritted teeth said, "I was told to take you alive, but you're crap. You're dead now, Marlin."

Ryker went to him, sidestepped a kick and landed one into Marlin's belly. He went double but still held onto his attache case.

Ryker lifted him up over his head and began to twirl him around till the sky became a dizzying swirl. Then Ryker twirled till he reached the edge and without thinking any more about it he heaved his cargo over.

"That for you, killer. There'll be no trial. You may have escaped the chair, but you didn't escape Ryker."

As Marlin went down he let out a piercing scream that echoed against the walls of the skyscrapers and drowned out Ryker's words. The last thing Ryker screamed before the body hit the street below was, "That's for you killer, a fitting end for a devil like you."

Ryker was exhausted, scratched up, blood pouring from his mouth and face. He looked up at the late winter sun and smiled. It would be a beautiful day.

Marlin's attache case, the one with the money in it, that Ryker did not know about, fell down more slowly. It hit the walls of tall buildings and after a few hits, each of which broke its fall, it came open and hundreds of nice new fifties showered across the sky and fell on Forty-Second Street and Times Square.

The people below looked up at the manna and screamed in surprise and joy, fought with each other to grab the money and laughed and chattered. Cars stopped, people got out and amid the traffic went down on all fours to grab bills that had floated under cars.

The people laughed in a festive holiday mood. It was truly an unexpected and fine day. Ryker laughed when he saw this.

RYKER SERIES
by Nelson DeMille

Ryker is the big city cop who hates the human garbage he dumps in the slammer just a little more than the fixers and the crooked fuzz who send him out to do society's dirty work.

Ryker #5   LB266ZK $1.25
THE CHILD KILLER
Jack Garrison
A psychopathic killer who preyed on children was on the loose in New York. Ryker's job was to nail the maniac before he panicked the city. But he made one near fatal mistake—he became emotionally involved in the case.

Ryker #4
THE AGENT OF DEATH   LB219ZK $1.25
A crazed CIA assassin, a master of torture who did his dirty work on the Viet Cong, is loose in the city with gruesome and blood curdling vengeance as his goal.

Ryker #3
THE TERRORISTS   LB207ZK   #$1.25
The American Freedom Army was a group of degenerate hoodlums whose "military operations" included kidnapping, robbery, arson and murder. Ryker had to crush the guerillas before they paralyzed the city with fear.

Ryker #2
THE HAMMER OF GOD   LB212ZK $1.25
A mad monk was brutally murdering innocent girls. He stripped them, bound them and drove a wooden stake through their hearts. Ryker's most savage case.

Ryker #1
THE SNIPER   LB194ZK $1.25
A Vietnam veteran, a psychopathic killer with a sniper rifle and a grudge, was loose in the city. Ryker had to track him down.

THE HUNTER
Crime Series
by Ralph Hayes

The Hunter is John Yard, who left the U.S. Army to make a new life on the grassy plains of Kenya in East Africa. But vicious and crooked elements keep beckoning him back to civilization.

Hunter #1
SCAVENGER KILL　　　　　LB224ZK　$1.25

An explosive new series. U.S. Army Colonel John Yard, sickened by war, becomes a hunter in East Africa. But even there the evils of the world crowd in on him. John Yard—The Hunter—kills for good.

Hunter #3
A TASTE OF BLOOD　　　　LB243ZK　$1.25

Seven men and one woman survived the crash in the African swampland. One by one they began to die. That was when they realized that one of them was a killer.

The Hunter #4
TRACK OF THE BEAST　　　LB262ZK　$1.25
Ralph Hayes

Uganda is in the grip of a psychotic politician. John Yard and Moses Ngala set out to break the bloody chains of his tryanny.

The Hunter #5　　　　　　　LB277ZK　$1.25
THE DEADLY PREY
Ralph Hayes

In Appalachia a sadistic maniac was developing a deadly virus and using human beings as his guinea pigs. One of these young men died horribly. When John Yard, The Hunter, looked into the case he realized there was nothing the law could do, so he took over the vengeance himself.

SHARPSHOOTER SERIES

by Bruno Rossi

When the Mafia murdered his parents and brother, Johnny Rock swore to avenge their deaths. He launched a one man war against the Syndicate.

Sharpshooter #9
STILETTO LB196NK 95¢

Johnny Rock was after a million gallons of hijacked gasoline. The Mafia had it. He blew the whole thing sky high.

Sharpshooter #8
NO QUARTER GIVEN LB187NK 95¢

The closer Johnny Rock got to the mob's crime empire the more it reeked of crooked Washington politicians and high-level payoffs.

Sharpshooter #7
HEADCRUSHER LB176NK 95¢

The setting is the seedy side of New York's Times Square—the Mafia controlled porn shops and massage parlors. Johnny Rock moves in to clean up in his usual lethal way.

Sharpshooter #6
MUZZLE BLAST LB170NK 95¢

Johnny Rock traveled to Cape Cod to shoot up the Mafia's control of the heroin trade. The resulting duel between him and the Massachusetts Organization makes a bloody story that holds readers on edge until the savage end.

Sharpshooter #13
SAVAGE SLAUGHTER LB244ZK $1.25

Johnny Rocco takes after a brothel baron and blasts the whole underworld to blazes. Action packed.

Sharpshooter #14
LAS VEGAS VENGEANCE　　　**LB261ZK**　**$1.25**
Bruno Rossi

Johnny Rock went to Vegas to play—and ended up gambling with his life.

Sharpshooter #4
THE WORST WAY TO DIE　　　**LB156NK**　**95¢**

The gang chieftain of the most powerful Mafia family thought he had a death grip on millions. But he hadn't counted on the stone determination of the Sharpshooter.

The Sharpshooter #15　　　**LB276ZK**　**$1.25**
A DIRTY WAY TO DIE
Bruno Rossi

Mafia henchmen haven't been able to kill Johnny Rock—The Sharpshooter—so they frame him for the submachine gun murder of a retarded boy.

MAFIA DEATH WATCH　　　**LB286ZK**　**$1.25**
Bruno Rossi

A young girl in Detroit wanted to get out of prostitution, but the Mafia refused, and killed her horribly. Johnny Rock heard about the killing and was persuaded to clean out the nest of Mafia rats that acted as pimps for The Murder Capital of the World.

Sharpshooter #11
TRIGGERMAN　　　**LB229ZK**　**$1.25**

Out of jail, Mafia mobster Rick Tattilo figured to take up where he left off, with dope and prostitution. But Johnny Rocco, The Sharpshooter, had other plans for him.

Sharpshooter #12
SCARFACED KILLER　　　**LB235ZK**　**$1.25**

When gold is discovered in a small Oklahoma town the Mafia moves in and takes over. Then Johnny Rock shows up and all hell breaks loose.

CHERRY DELIGHT SERIES

by Glen Chase

Cherry Delight is the star detective of N.Y.M.P.H.O. (New York Mafia Prosecution and Harassment Organization). She's voluptuous, luscious and deadly.

Cherry Delight #18
HANG LOOSE   LB233ZK $1.25

The Mafia was out to control the wildest sex potion ever invented by a mad scientist. Cherry wasn't going to let them get away with it.

Cherry Delight #17
TREASURE CHEST   LB220ZK $1.25

Cherry discovers a Mafia plot to reduce America's great art collections to the paint on the walls.

Cherry Delight #16
BUSTED   LB214ZK $1.25

There's buried treasure off the Florida coast. But Cherry has to bury a few hit men before she can sample the baubles.

Cherry Delight #15
WHAT A WAY TO GO   LB208ZK $1.25

In this spicy romp Cherry trails mob men through the Haitian jungle.

Cherry Delight #14
IN A PINCH   LB202ZK $1.25

This time Cherry takes on a partner—beautiful Rhoda. Together, they go to Italy and land jobs as bellydancers in order to track the Mafia.

Cherry Delight #13
OVER THE HUMP   LB195ZK $1.25

In this caper Cherry fights the Mafia across the North African desert. The fact that she gets caught in a Berber sex orgy doesn't faze her.

Cherry Delight #12
FIRE IN THE HOLE   LB175ZK $1.25

The Mafia is trying to muscle in on the oil industry and take advantage of the energy crisis. Cherry stops them with a body block.

Cherry Delight #10
MADE IN JAPAN   LB157ZK $1.25

The thugs in Tokyo get a bang out of Cherry as she causes havoc in their Oriental works.

Cherry Delight #9
THE JERSEY BOUNCE   LB151ZK $1.25

Cherry gets caught in a vicious power play between an ailing Godfather and a rebel Mafia thug. She lands a job as a topless waitress, ready to bounce the Mafia men off the map.

Cherry Delight #8
HOT ROCKS   LB143ZK $1.25

Cherry fights to stop the Mafia's stranglehold on the international diamond market.

Cherry Delight #7
CHUCK YOU, FARLEY!   LB138ZK $1.25

Nazi-trained counterfeiters are pitted against a double-dealing American named Charley Farley—but Cherry deals the blows.

Cherry Delight #19
IN A BIND   LB242ZK $1.25

Cherry is framed for murder, but that's *one* thing she won't take lying down.

Cherry Delight #21
MEXICAN STANDOFF   LB260ZK $1.25
Glen Chase
The Mob was growing opium in Mexico. Cherry's job was to smoke them out.

Cherry Delight #5
CRACK SHOT   LB125ZK $1.25
Cherry is off on another sexy thriller when two Mafia families squabble over control of the lucrative sex film industry. Plenty of squeezing goes on all around as Cherry elbows in on the battle.

Cherry Delight #4
UP YOUR ANTE   LB119ZK $1.25
Cherry relies on her set of pistols, a load of dynamite, and her faithful bazooka to blow a hole through the British gambling racket.

Cherry Delight #22   LB265ZK $1.25
THE BIG BANKROLL
Glen Chase
Cherry Delight, star agent of N.Y.M.P.H.O. (New York Mafia Harassment Organization) runs into a new type of Mafia hood—members of an underworld think tank. Also a few sported some very kinky tastes—and though Cherry is not one to balk at kinkiness she did object when it led to killing.

Cherry Delight #23   LB274ZK $1.25
LIGHTS! ACTION! MURDER!
Glen Chase

Strong arm men are muscling in on the movies, and a maverick producer asks Cherry Delight for help. Masquerading as Coco Madrid, Hollywood's newest sensational skin-flick superstar, Cherry has to take it all off in order to take the gang on.

SCIENCE FICTION/OCCULT

THE ISLAND OF DR. MOREAU
H.G. Wells LB211NK 95¢

Dr. Moreau had created a hideous race of creatures. For years he had flogged, tortured and killed at will —but a revolt was brewing among the "things."

TIME IS THE SIMPLEST THING
Clifford D. Simak LB198NK 95¢

Millions of light years from Earth, the Telepathic Explorer found his mind possessed by an alien creature.

THE EIGHTY MINUTE HOUR LB237ZK $1.25
Brian Aldiss

"There is no way to describe the mad sci-fi genius of Brian Aldiss, except to say that he is Joyce, Huxley, Waugh on a pot party..." Edward L. Harris, author of The Giants of Science Fiction.

WATCHERS OF THE DARK LB275NK $.95
Lloyd Biggle, Jr.

Total destruction hits planet after planet, and Earth is next. Insanity spreads like a plague. Jan Darzek was summoned to identify and halt the dreadful weapon called "The Dark." Then he felt his own sanity slipping away....

KYRIK FIGHTS THE DEMON WORLD LB284NK $.95
Gardner F. Fox

When Kyrik—warlock warrior—finds a dying man and a bloody parchment map, he is drawn into a whirlwind of evil in which demon lords contend for all Terra.

LEISURE PERSONALITY SERIES

JACKIE   LB281KK $1.75
Hedda Lyons Watney

The life and loves of the most famous and desirable woman in the world. Jackie Kennedy Onassis, beautiful, fabulously wealthy yet somehow tragic, has left an indelible impression on her time. Yet despite the glare of publicity that surrounds her, she remains a mystery. What is she *really* like? Will she marry again? And who?

ROBERT REDFORD   LB291DK $1.50
David Hanna

Here is an intimate behind-the-scenes look at a sensitive, intelligent man who came up in his profession through patience, talent and lots of sexy charm. There's much more to the man behind the Redford image than is visible on the screen—and **Robert Redford: The Superstar Nobody Knows** attacks and dispels that mystery.

STREISAND   LB298DK $1.50
Jonathan Black

Barbra Streisand, an overnight sensation, went on to become the biggest superstar in show business. This is her story!

BARBARA WALTERS: LB306DK $1.50
TODAY'S WOMAN
Jason Bonderoff

This is the fascinating life story of the most famous woman in television. It tells of her triumphs and her tragedies; of how the news writer became an international celebrity and a household world.

LEISURE BOOKS
P.O. Box 2301
Norwalk, Conn. 06852

Name

Address

City

State   Zip

Please send check, cash or money order. No stamps. No C.O.D.

Book Number_____ Price_____
Book Number_____ Price_____
Book Number_____ Price_____
Book Number_____ Price_____
Book Number_____ Price_____
Book Number_____ Price_____

Add 25¢ per book to help cover cost of postage and handling. Buy 4 or more books and we will cover all costs. Allow 4 weeks for delivery.